The Darkest Veil

by Catherine Cavendish

Suzie leaped up and snapped the light switch on. We blinked in the brightness and stared at the broken glass on the floor.

"What the hell happened?" Suzie asked. "Who moved that bloody glass?"

I shook my head and looked around at the shocked, white faces of my housemates.

Diana recovered first. "I don't believe any of us did. Alice, what did Lena say we should do when something goes wrong?"

I struggled to collect my thoughts. "She said...we can do one of two things. We can either stop. Well, I suppose we have anyway. But we could start again if we choose to. Or we could call it a night."

"I prefer that option," Diana said, rubbing her hands together. "Does anyone else feel cold all of a sudden?"

I nodded and hugged myself. The room had grown chilly in the last few minutes and my breath misted when I spoke. "Shall we see what Vicky's got?"

Vicky had been forming words from the letters I had shouted out and stared at her notebook.

I prompted her. "Vicky?"

She looked up at me. "Oh, you're all going to love this," she said.

"What do you mean?" I asked. "Does any of it make sense?"

"It makes sense all right."

"Then tell us!" Suzie's impatience bordered on anger.

Vicky glared at her. "Fine. It says 'We are the thirteen. We are one. He is coming for you. He will take you with him.'"

Dedication

For Colin, without whom...
and in memory of Susan Roebuck—writer, artist, friend. Lost to
us too soon

Acknowledgments

Julia Kavan, writer and indispensable reader of my early drafts. Thank you as always.

The 'Two Davids'—David Dodd and David Niall Wilson. Thank you for being great publishers. I love working with you guys.

And to you, reading this story. Thank you. I hope you enjoy this tale, which has an element of 'confessions of a misspent youth' in it. Suffice it to say, don't mess with Ouijas, you may end up with more than you bargained for...

'When death's darkest veil draws over you, then shall shadows weep'.

Chapter One

The moment I stepped across the battered and unloved threshold, the house welcomed me. It led me in, wrapped me in a cocoon of softness and told me I had come home.

My name is Alice Lorrimer and in September 1972, I had recently left my English High School with a clutch of half-decent exam results and an unshakeable belief that, like all eighteen-year-olds, I could change the world simply by being in it. How I would accomplish that, as a humble bank clerk, wasn't yet clear to me.

I had unpacked my few belongings and made up my bed when a smart rap on my door heralded the arrival of a pixie of a woman who looked a few years older than me. She wore her bleached blonde hair short, sported a broad grin, and held a lit cigarette between her fingers.

"Hello, new girl, I'm Suzie. I live in number five upstairs." The broad Leeds accent was embellished with the gravelly throatiness of the chain-smoker.

"Hi, I'm Alice," I said. I gauged my housemate to be in her late twenties. Thirty maybe, but no more. She scanned the room, grinning broadly as she saw the clutch of novels on the mantelpiece, which doubled as a temporary bookshelf.

"You like the Angelique books, too," Suzie said. "Imagine being her. All those adventures and handsome men lusting after her. All I've ever done is a string of dead-end jobs and divorced a bastard of a husband." She laughed, the raucousness ending in a cough. "God, I must quit these cigs."

She pointed the offending "cig" at me and I handed her the ashtray I had laid on the small dining table. Suzie mashed her cigarette up and handed the receptacle and its massacred contents back to me. I set it down again.

"I've only just moved to Leeds," I said. "I'm from York."

She raised her eyebrows. "You'll find a bit of a difference here, love. Leeds is much more modern—and a hell of a lot noisier. Better nightlife here, too."

Apparently forgetting her earlier resolve to quit, Suzie reached into the pocket of her jeans and pulled out a slightly battered box of Embassy Regal. She offered me one, but I shook my head. I only ever smoked menthol.

Suzie lit up, inhaled and blew out a cloud of acrid smoke. "So what do you think of the house then?"

"I've really not seen it properly yet, but the bathroom and kitchen seem okay. Is there a cleaning rota?"

Suzie let out a hoarse belly laugh. "Cleaning? That kitchen's lucky if someone remembers to empty the waste bin. That's why I live in number five. I've got my own kitchen. I can keep my germs to myself and not pick up anyone else's. Can't stand congealed grease and dirty cookers." She wrinkled her nose. "As for the bathroom...at least people seem to keep *that* relatively tidy. I shove a load of bleach down the toilet once a week, so anything you can do to help will be appreciated."

"Okay."

Suzie took another drag of her cigarette. "Anyway, I'd better let you get sorted. If you need anything, knock on my door."

"Thanks, Suzie."

She put her hand on the doorknob, then hesitated. "A piece of advice. This house is a bit...well...different."

"Different?"

"Yes. It..." I waited as she searched for the words. To my surprise, she advanced towards me. Instinctively I took a step back. "It's okay, Alice. I didn't mean to startle you. I don't want to talk too loudly, that's all."

She glanced behind her. I followed her gaze, but saw nothing. She flicked the ash of her cigarette into the ashtray and took a deep breath. "When you got here this afternoon, did you feel anything?"

"I don't quite follow..."

"Did you feel like you were being drawn into the house?"

I searched my memory. "I did feel the house had a welcoming atmosphere. Sort of warm and homely."

"Like it wrapped you up in a blanket?"

That described my impression perfectly. It had felt like someone had wrapped me in the softest fleece. Comforting. Protective. I hadn't thought much to it then, but now Suzie had mentioned it...

Suzie smiled. "Oh, don't mind me. I don't mean anything by it. Be aware, that's all. Things happen here sometimes."

"What sort of things?"

Suzie opened her mouth to speak, shook her head and said nothing. She stared down at her hands. Her knuckles were white from clenching—a gesture at odds with the smile which seemed pasted on her face as she looked back up at me and our eyes met.

"Ignore me," she said. "Too much imagination. My mam always warned me it would get me into trouble. Nice to meet you, Alice."

Suzie crossed the room and shut the door behind her before I could respond.

That night, as I lay in bed, the orange glow of the streetlights cast deep fingers of shadow across the room. I mulled over what Suzie had said. How she had seemed almost scared to speak about the house. But why? Maybe simply winding up the new girl. Yes, that would be the most likely explanation. I turned over and fell asleep.

"Come and join us, Alice," Suzie said. "We're all going down the Yarby for a couple of halves."

Suzie leaned against a large cupboard in the kitchen the other four of us shared. The mixed smells of yesterday's tinned curry, vinegar from someone's fish and chips, and the usual sour smell from the sink meant I was always glad to get out of there. Saturday tomorrow and I had already resolved to buy a big bottle of bleach and some rubber gloves.

Vicky and Diana, two of my other housemates, were also there. Only the quiet little mouse, Anita, in number four was missing. I had barely exchanged two words with her as she scurried up to her bedsit.

I pulled a face. "I don't get paid 'til next week and I'm broke."

Vicky tossed back her unruly auburn curls. "We're all in the same boat," she said. "That's what the cupboard's for." She pulled open the tall doors of a large, solid cupboard I hadn't yet investigated. Shelf upon shelf jam-packed with bottles that had contained beer, cider, lemonade. All had one thing in common--returning them to the shop meant getting money back.

Vicky started handing bottles to Diana and Suzie who had a collection of large plastic sacks to pile them into. "We do this every couple of months," she said. "We usually get enough to buy at least one round of drinks, sometimes more."

"Great idea." I took a bottle off Vicky and added it to the others. "But I feel guilty. I haven't contributed to this."

"Ah, but you will," Diana said, tucking a strand of her short black hair behind her ears. "By next month you'll have added your fair share to the cupboard. Each of us has had a free ride the first time."

We piled the bottles into the sacks. A wave of happiness filled me. I felt accepted by these girls and, as a naturally shy person who found it difficult to make new friends, this boosted my confidence. In my new life, I could be whoever I chose to be. They knew nothing of me before this week. I could mold myself into an entirely new character if I wanted. I didn't have to be shy Alice anymore. I could be gregarious, outgoing Alice. I smiled and carried on helping my new friends until we had emptied the cupboard. We carried a sack in each hand and clanked our way over to the Off License.

The shopkeeper greeted the girls like an old friend.

"Off to the pub, I see." He smiled.

Suzie hoisted her bags up on the counter. "Hello, Mr. Dent. Yes, just dropping off the empties. This is Alice, by the way. She moved in this month."

Mr. Dent held out his hand and I shook it. He looked to be in his fifties, with graying hair slicked back and shiny with Brylcreem. His smile revealed teeth stained by years of smoking, but genuine warmth shone through his eyes.

"A pleasure to meet you, Alice. Don't let these girls lead you astray."

"Mr. Dent!" Suzie exclaimed in mock horror. "Us? Lead her astray? Whatever can you be thinking. Pure as the driven snow, us lot."

Mr. Dent laughed. "Yes. After a cartload of monkeys have driven through it."

He handed over our money to Diana. "There you are, girls, enjoy your evening. Don't get too drunk now."

"Strictly Coke," Vicky said, her expression serious before she broke out into a broad grin.

"Of course, Vicky," Mr. Dent said and winked at me.

We left the shop giggling like schoolgirls, linked arms and crossed the road.

An atmosphere smogged by tobacco smoke, loud chatter, raucous laughter and the incessant clinking of glasses met us at the door of the Yarborough Arms.

We squeezed our way past throngs of the young and the not-so-young. A couple was moving away from a table, well-placed near the bar, and Diana demonstrated why she had gained medals for athletics at school, by ducking and diving her way forward before a final short sprint saw her grab the table a mere second ahead of a middle-aged man. He brandished a pint of bitter and a newly acquired scowl. Diana smiled sweetly at him and he stomped away, muttering under his breath.

I sat down with Diana while Vicky and Suzie disappeared into the melee to fight their way to the bar. Ten minutes later they were back with a clutch of half pints of cider for Diana and me, and lager and lime for themselves.

Cigarettes were exchanged, ashtrays started filling up. I took my turn braving the madding crowd at the bar, with Suzie, who didn't believe in waiting and had the decibels to ensure she didn't need to. "What do I have to do to get some service here!" she yelled. "Oy." She elbowed her way in front of a burly man with a dragon tattoo on his forearm. "I got here first, buster, wait your turn."

I held my breath. Surely this six-foot-square giant wasn't

going to take that from a five-foot blonde with attitude? But to my amazement he moved away.

Suzie shot in with her order. "Two halves of lager and lime and two halves of cider please."

"How did you do that?" I asked when we returned to the others.

Diana grinned. "That's Suzie. She doesn't take any shit from anyone."

Suzie nodded. "It comes from growing up in the roughest part of Leeds with three older brothers. Doesn't work every time, though. That's when I duck. Being short, I can squeeze under them."

"I've got a lot to learn," I said, handing around my St Moritz menthols. "I never thought I'd lived a sheltered life, but now I think I must have."

"Ah well, we're not posh like those York toffs," Suzie said, smiling at me. "You'll soon get the hang of us."

"Speak for yourself, Baxter," Vicky said. "We're not all from Hunslet. I'm from Wakefield." She winked at me.

A warm glow spread over me as I laughed with my new friends. It had taken a lot for me to leave my comfortable home where I'd lived since babyhood. My mother had wept. My father had tried to persuade me to stay, but I had been determined to push myself, to get out into the big, wide world, earn my own living and make my own mistakes, away from the cozy cocoon my parents had wrapped around me.

It was the Seventies. A great time to be single, free, and an adult. Women's Liberation yelled at full throttle and, while I didn't bring myself to burn my bra, I certainly wasn't prepared to settle for a dead-end job. I wouldn't waste my time waiting for the right man to whisk me off my feet, stick a ring on my finger, and chain me to the kitchen sink for the rest of my life.

"But Alice," my mother had said, putting her arms around me. She gave me a tight hug and then held me at arm's length. Tears glistened in her eyes. "How will you cope on your own?"

"Mum, I'm eighteen. I can take care of myself. It would be the same if I was going off to college."

"No, it wouldn't. At least at college there are people looking out for you. Leeds is a big city for a young girl all on her own."

"But I won't be on my own. I'll have work colleagues at the bank and I'm moving into a house with four other girls. I'm going to do this, Mum, and I'm going to make it work. Please be happy for me."

She sighed, hesitated, and then nodded. She knew I wouldn't change my mind. I had inherited my stubborn streak from her.

Already I had drifted away from the schoolfriends I had known for years. They had either stayed put or gone off to Teacher Training College or University. As far as I knew, I was the only one of us who had decided to strike out on her own. In a couple of weeks, I already had more in common with the three people sitting around the table with me now than I did with any of them.

"So, Alice," Diana exhaled a cloud of smoke. "How's the new job shaping up?"

"It's okay," I said, unsure whether I meant it or not. "There's a lot to learn, but I'm getting to grips with it. I think so anyway."

"I always reckon it takes a good six months to get yourself bedded in," Vicky said. "I've been in this job a year and I swear it took me two days to find the ladies' loo."

Suzie laughed. "I've had jobs that didn't even last two days."

"Yes, Suzie," Vicky said. "But you make your mind up within an hour whether you're going to like the job or not. You don't give them a chance."

"Life's too short for boring jobs." Suzie lit up yet another cigarette, inhaled and coughed. "God, these bloody cigs. Anyway, there's always another job. This latest one's not so bad. The boss stays in his office most of the time. He drinks. Spends the afternoon lying on this big couch of his, snoring his head off."

"I've had a boss like that." Diana said. "Absolute nightmare. No point talking to him after lunch, you'd never get one word of sense out of him. In the end, he got fired when someone from Head Office turned up unexpectedly and found him passed out cold, with an empty bottle of Scotch next to him."

I smiled. "I don't think I'll have that problem. My boss is a tyrant, but at least he's a sober one."

"Any decent blokes in your office?" Suzie asked.

"Some, but they're the married ones. There's this guy called David who is single, but you kind of know why. He's a total drip. Keeps making snide comments and staring at my chest." My flesh crawled with an army of ants as an image of greasy-haired, shiny-suited David Lipscomb flashed into my mind.

"Have you got a boyfriend, Alice?" Vicky asked.

I shook my head. "Not now. I did have back home, but we split up in the summer. It wasn't really going anywhere so it was probably for the best. He's gone off to University. Going to be an engineer. How about you?"

"No. Mick and I called it a day last month. I couldn't trust him after I caught him chatting up a girl in the pub. He didn't know I'd turned up and I caught him writing his phone number on her arm."

"Ouch!" I said.

"Ouch, indeed. Especially when I landed a punch in his face."

Suzie giggled. "She broke his nose."

"What? Really?"

Vicky nodded. "Bruised my knuckles. They hurt for days."

Even through the cacophony of noise around us, heads turned to see where the guffaws were coming from.

When we eventually recovered ourselves, Diana wiped tears from her cheeks. "I know who I'd employ if I ever needed a bodyguard. Vicky, you're hired." She raised her glass. "And now a toast, ladies. To Alice, our latest housemate. May she spend many happy months at number four."

The following Friday, we had all been paid, and Suzie joined us in the kitchen. She grinned and shook a little package wrapped in tin foil at us.

Diana patted her on her back. "You got it. Good girl!"

"Got what?" I asked.

"Look, don't tell Anita," Suzie said, "because she'll probably do something stupid like call the police."

All sorts of thoughts collided in my mind, until I settled on one. "You mean?"

Suzie nodded. "A nice little package of hash for us to enjoy this evening. Come to my flat around eight. Bring a bottle." She raced upstairs.

"Have you ever tried it?" Vicky asked.

I shook my head. "No. Never. You?"

"It's the only time I smoke, but not often. It's a great feeling though. Getting high."

We were interrupted by the sound of someone coming down the stairs. Diana stood nearest the door. "It's Anita."

Vicky briefly put her finger to her lips. "Hi Anita," she said. "How are you?"

"Okay, thanks." I could barely hear her.

"Got any plans for the weekend?" I asked.

She responded with a mere shake of her head. Out of sight of Anita, I exchanged glances with Diana, who rolled her eyes.

Anita opened her small cupboard, removed a packet of crisps, and closed it again. Then she half-ran out of the room and back up the stairs.

"She couldn't wait to get out of here," I said.

Diana nodded. "I don't know what makes that girl tick. You can never have a conversation with her. Maybe it's shyness, or that she simply doesn't like us."

"Shyness, I reckon," I said.

"You're probably right," Diana said, "Shame she doesn't make more of an effort to overcome it though."

I nearly told her how hard that could be. How every day I had to play the part of a self-confident young woman called Alice Lorrimer. Then I realized. Making the effort to reinvent myself had paid off. It felt like *me* now. Not simply some role play. My mind filled with a sense of achievement.

"What are you smiling at?" Diana asked.

"Oh, it's … it's Friday evening. No work 'til Monday. That's plenty to smile about." I slapped some cheese between two slices of buttered bread and ate my sandwich.

Later, the four of us lounged on cushions on the floor of Suzie's flat. The room contained an unfamiliar aroma. Sweet, a little heavy, clinging.

Suzie took a long drag on the misshapen joint. "Ah, the

sweet, sweet smell of Mary Jane." She passed the weed to me. "Come along, my hash virgin. Try some of that. It's good stuff."

Hesitantly, I took the joint between my thumb and fore-finger, raised it to my lips and took a drag. My mouth filled with the acrid taste of tobacco tempered with another taste that mirrored the aroma around me.

"Draw the smoke in deeply," Diana said. "Hold onto it, don't exhale straightaway."

I tried, but unused to unfiltered, non-menthol cigarettes, I could only manage a couple of seconds before I spluttered. I passed the joint onto Diana. Next time around, I passed. I resolved to try again another day. Especially when, all around me, my new friends grew pleasantly mellow.

I poured myself a glass of dry white wine and took a gulp. My taste buds objected to the acidity of the cheap alcohol, but a couple of glasses later and I felt as relaxed as my housemates.

Vicky interrupted my thoughts. "So, Suzie, has anything been happening in your flat? You've not mentioned any weird noises for weeks."

"A bit of tapping at the window but nothing much else."

"Maybe whatever it is has gone away," Diana said. "Oh, sorry, Alice, you probably don't know what we're talking about, do you?"

Before I could answer, Suzie stepped in. "I told her a bit on the day she moved in."

"Have you any idea what's causing the noises?" I asked.

Everyone shook their heads. "Haven't a clue," Diana said. "It only seems to happen in Suzie's room."

"Well, not *in* my room exactly. More on the roof and at the window, and then it's the bedsit not the kitchen. Never in the daylight either. Always in the middle of the night or early hours of the morning." She stood up. "Anyone else got the munchies?" Diana and Vicky nodded. "I've got a load of crisps and stuff in the kitchen. I'll go and get them."

She returned quickly and handed out potato chips and peanuts. She, Diana, and Vicky attacked theirs with a ven-geance. I opened a packet of salted peanuts and munched away steadily.

"About those noises you heard, Suzie," I said. "Do you believe in the supernatural?"

Suzie smiled. "I didn't used to, but I've got no explanation for any of it, so I don't know now."

"Have you ever thought of trying to talk to it?" I asked. "Like a séance?"

Suzie stared for a moment, then burst out laughing. "Are you kidding?"

"No," Diana said. "Hang on a minute. Alice has got a point."

"Are you serious?" Vicky stared at her and then at me.

Diana leaned forward. "Why not?"

"It's all a load of mumbo jumbo," Suzie said.

Diana nodded. "Maybe, but you would have said anything supernatural was a load of mumbo jumbo until those noises started."

The smile froze on Suzie's face. Vicky continued to stare, her mouth slightly open as if she felt she had somehow wandered into a parallel universe.

Diana turned to me. "Alice, do you know how séances work? Would you be able to set it up or whatever?"

I shook my head. "I can always get a book out of the library. There's bound to be one."

"Great. What do you think, Suzie? At the worst we could have a bit of fun. If there really is something in it, you could finally get some answers."

Suzie puffed her cigarette for a moment. "Oh, why the hell not? It'll be a laugh."

"You lot really *are* serious, aren't you?" Vicky said. "I can't believe we're having this conversation."

"Oh, don't get all sensible and po-faced," Suzie said. "It's a bit of fun, that's all. Nothing's going to happen. Let's face it, it's a load of nonsense."

Vicky seemed about to respond but settled for shaking her head and sipping her drink.

"Will you join in?" I asked her.

She blinked her clear green eyes, then a smile twitched the corners of her lips. "Oh, what the hell? What are you going to do? Use a Ouija board?"

"How do you do that?" I asked.

"You'll need to make a circle with letters of the alphabet, the words 'Yes' and 'No' and 'Goodbye' I think." The rest of us stared at her.

Suzie said what we were all thinking. "For someone who's skeptical about this stuff, you certainly seem to know a lot."

Vicky grinned. "I read Dennis Wheatley and a load of other scary books in my teens. I grew out of it."

The wine ran out and we headed for the pub—noisy and crowded as ever. We managed to grab the only available table while its previous occupants were still getting ready to move. Once Diana had brought the drinks, we carried on where we left off.

"I've got a pack of Lexicon cards," I said. "That'll give us the letters of the alphabet."

Vicky nodded. "Good. We'll need a table, a sturdy glass tumbler, and four chairs. Oh, do you think we should invite Anita?"

Suzie pulled a face. "Why bother? She always says no whenever we invite her anywhere. Strange girl."

"She told me she's thinking of becoming a nun," Diana said.

"You're kidding," Suzie said. "*Really?*"

Diana crossed her forefinger across her heart. "I swear it. I was washing my dishes a few days ago and she sidled in, the way she does. Gave me the fright of my life. I didn't hear her."

Vicky shivered. "She gives me the creeps."

"She said 'sorry' in that little mouse voice of hers, and when I'd put my heart back in my chest, she started talking to me. It must be the first time I've ever had anything resembling a conversation with her. Anyway, she told me that's what she's planning to do."

"You mean, she just came out with it?" I said.

"Pretty much, yes. I can't remember how we got onto the subject. I may have asked her what she does for a living, but if I did, I can't remember what she told me, except she wants to take holy orders."

"Probably best not to invite her to a séance then." I failed to suppress a fit of giggles—and so did my friends.

Vicky picked up her purse from the seat beside her. "My round," she said. "Same again?"

"I'll come with you," Suzie said.

"Oh, good, I could do with our resident homing missile." We laughed and the two left.

Diana stubbed out her cigarette and leaned closer towards me. "Suzie may be laughing about it this evening, but I've seen her genuinely terrified. She woke and saw something in her room one night. A tall man, dressed in black, with long white hair. She told us he stood in the middle of her room and stared at her. She didn't dare move. Then he faded from sight. That's when she screamed. I came racing up the stairs. I think I was the only one in at the time. She opened her door and practically fainted in my arms. I just caught her in time and broke her fall. The next day she said she must have dreamed it but, I tell you, if that's true, it was one hell of a realistic nightmare."

"I think if that had been me, I'd have moved out." I shivered. "Has anything like that happened since?"

"I don't think so. But plenty of other stuff has. Suzie reckons there's a logical explanation that she hasn't come up with yet. Maybe that's right. Maybe the footsteps on the roof are those of a bird. The window tapping, too. I've known seagulls do that. At work we had one that used to come and tap on the window every morning for weeks."

Suzie and Vicky returned, bearing drinks.

"I've been telling Alice about that man you saw in your room. The one that wasn't really there."

Suzie smiled and reached for her cigarettes. She offered the pack around and then lit one. "Bad dream. I get them sometimes."

"Anyway," I said, "About this séance—"

Vicky interrupted. "I'm having second thoughts again."

Suzie gave an exasperated sigh. "Oh, come on, Vick, it's just a bit of fun."

Vicky shook her head. "Dennis Wheatley always said not to mess about with Ouija boards and summon spirits. He urged people not to do it because you might get more than you bargained for. Let in something really evil and then not be able to control it."

I spoke up. "I reckon Dennis Wheatley was a pretty good salesman. It's simple psychology. Tell someone something is bad for them, that they shouldn't do it and they immediately want to give it a go. Oh, and by the way, they'd better buy one of his books to find out how it's done."

"Alice has got a point there," Diana said. "I vote we do it anyway. But I won't buy one of his books."

"I'm up for it," I said.

"Me, too," said Suzie.

We all looked at Vicky who shifted in her seat. "Oh, all right then, if you must, but we'd better do our homework first and make sure we do everything we need to in order to protect ourselves."

Suzie, who had taken a gulp of her drink, spluttered, spraying us with lager and lime. She wiped her mouth with the back of her hand. "Sorry. Didn't mean to do that. Vicky, come on. Nothing is going to happen, right? Not unless we make it happen by pushing the glass and we must agree that none of us will do that."

We all nodded. None of us would do that.

"You're holding a séance?" Jackie, one of my new colleagues at the bank, passed me a digestive biscuit as she, another girl called Lena, and I sat in the coffee room on our morning break.

"Have you ever done it before?" Lena asked.

I shook my head. "One of my housemates read up a bit about it."

"You need to be careful," Lena said.

"Oh, it's a lot of nonsense really," I said, but Lena's expression grew more serious.

"No, I mean it," she said. "If you mess around with this stuff, you can unleash something you really don't want around."

"You sound as if you know all about it," I said.

"Oh, she does," Jackie said. "She's a bit psychic, aren't you Lena?"

Lena shrugged her shoulders. "I see things sometimes. Shadowy things. I'm never quite sure if they're real or in my head."

"You knew when my brother was going to have an accident, even though you'd never met him."

"*Did* you?" I asked.

Lena nodded. "I had this image in my head of a teenage boy with a bicycle, and a car moving too quickly towards him. Someone screamed at him to get out of the way and he just caught the front bumper, but he was thrown clear."

"That's pretty much what happened a couple of hours later," Jackie said. "Lena warned me, but I didn't believe her, so I didn't ring my mum to tell her to keep Richie off the road. I won't make that mistake again."

"Somehow, I knew the boy I'd seen had a connection to Jackie."

"That's impressive," I said. "You wouldn't be able to come over to ours and conduct this séance for us, would you?"

Lena closed her eyes for a moment, then opened them. "No, I'm sorry, but I tell you what I *will* do. You bring those Lexicon cards in and, after work tomorrow, you, Jackie and me will have a short Ouija session here. That way, you'll know what to do."

"You're on," I said, excitement already building inside me. "Is there a specific reason why you don't want to come over to Suzie's flat?"

Lena hesitated. "Look, no offense, but you're going to do this anyway—with, or without my help. At least this way I can maybe show you some of the right ways of doing things. Help you protect yourselves. But, believe me when I say you would be far better advised to leave it all well alone." Without warning, she took hold of my hand and dropped it as if I had burned her. "There's something in your house, Alice. Something evil."

Chapter Two

"**B**e serious. Always say 'goodbye'. Never use it at home." Those were Lena's words of advice. Well, the third one had to be a non-starter. Where else could we use it *except* at home? We needed to find out if any spirits were hanging around there. They would hardly come and find us anywhere else.

Suzie's bedsit was under the eaves. Chintzy curtains hung at the single window which looked out over the road and across to the pub. For this evening, she had positioned a square table in the middle of the room and arranged four chairs around it. On the table, my Lexicon cards had been placed in a circle and Suzie had written 'Yes', 'No' and 'Goodbye' on some pieces of white card. A chunky tumbler stood upside down in the center.

"So what happened at your séance yesterday?" Diana asked as we sat down.

I shrugged. "Nothing much. The glass didn't move, but at least it gave Lena a chance to explain what we're supposed to do—and what to do if things go wrong."

"Wrong?" Suzie's voice trembled slightly. "What could go wrong exactly?"

"If a negative energy gets through."

Suzie gave a nervous giggle.

"I think we should probably get started, if we're going to do this." For the first time, Diana sounded unconvinced. Whether she transmitted that uncertainty to me, or whether I already felt it, I didn't know, but the time had come. Seeing the table set out that way, a niggling doubt began to snake its way up from the pit of my stomach. Lena's warning flashed through my mind. With sheer force of will, I suppressed it. Stuff and nonsense. That's all.

I took a deep breath. "Okay, Vicky, have you got a notebook and pen with you?"

She waved both at me.

"Great. As we agreed, you write everything down, but you don't need to touch the glass and you shouldn't ask any questions of anything that may make contact with us. The rest of us should each place a finger lightly on the glass."

Suzie coughed. "Should we turn the main light out or something? I could put the table lamp on so we can see the cards."

"Good idea," I said and Suzie obliged.

In the gloom, the atmosphere grew heavy in the room, not helped by a fug of tobacco smoke that hung in the air.

I took another deep breath and my heart beat a little faster.

We each rested the forefinger of one hand on the glass.

I cleared my throat. "Spirit, are you there?"

Another nervous giggle from Suzie.

"Ssshh." This from Diana. Next to me, Vicky waited, notebook open, pen poised.

I tried again, as Lena had advised. "Spirit, this is a safe place. Are you there?"

The glass trembled. I caught my breath as the floorboards creaked beneath our feet.

"Oh my God!" Suzie snatched her finger away. "Did you feel that?"

"Yes." My voice wobbled. "Please put your finger back, Suzie. We need our combined energies."

Suzie did so, without another word. No one else spoke. I guessed everyone was as taken aback as me. This hadn't happened yesterday evening.

"Spirit, is that you?" I asked.

The glass trembled again. Diana gasped. The tumbler seemed to be struggling to free itself. It began to shift. It slowly moved around the circle as if trying to familiarize itself with new surroundings. I watched in fascination as it snaked its way around the table.

The glass stopped abruptly, against one of the white cards. "Yes," I read. Vicky wrote it down.

Suzie, Vicky and Diana were silent. As leader, I had to ask

the questions. I had my next one ready, but with such a dry mouth, I could barely get the words out.

"Spirit, thank you for joining us. Please, will you spell out your name?"

The glass shot over to the white card on the other side of the circle—the one that read 'No'.

"But why won't it tell us its name?" Suzie asked.

The glass trembled violently, then darted around the board, stopping at letters and moving on so fast I could hardly keep up.

I called the letters to Vicky. She wrote them down. We were all breathing heavily as the glass moved faster and faster, gaining momentum all the time. Finally, with one massive tug, the tumbler flew off the table and smashed against the wall.

Suzie leaped up and snapped the light switch on. We blinked in the brightness and stared at the broken glass on the floor.

"What the hell happened?" Suzie asked. "Who moved that bloody glass?"

I shook my head and looked around at the shocked, white faces of my housemates.

Diana recovered first. "I don't believe any of us did. Alice, what did Lena say we should do when something goes wrong?"

I struggled to collect my thoughts. "She said…we can do one of two things. We can either stop. Well, I suppose we have anyway. But we could start again if we choose to. Or we could call it a night."

"I prefer that option," Diana said, rubbing her hands together. "Does anyone else feel cold all of a sudden?"

I nodded and hugged myself. The room had grown chilly in the last few minutes and my breath misted when I spoke. "Shall we see what Vicky's got?"

Vicky had been forming words from the letters I had shouted out and stared at her notebook.

I prompted her. "Vicky?"

She looked up at me. "Oh, you're all going to love this," she said.

"What do you mean?" I asked. "Does any of it make sense?"

"It makes sense all right."

"Then tell us!" Suzie's impatience bordered on anger.

Vicky glared at her. "Fine. It says 'We are the thirteen. We are one. He is coming for you. He will take you with him.'"

No one spoke as the seconds ticked by. Diana pushed her chair back and stood. "I'm going back to my room. I've had enough excitement for one night. Can I suggest that this is a one-off and we never do this again? I haven't a clue what the hell that was and, frankly, I don't think I want to know."

I nodded. The way I felt, nothing and no one would ever persuade me to tinker with forces I clearly didn't understand.

Vicky closed her notebook. "I told you what Dennis Wheatley said. Looks like he got it right."

Diana had her hand on the door handle.

"Just a sec," Suzie said, "Before you go, Diana, I'm going to ask the question we must all be wondering. Are you sure none of you moved that glass? I mean, we only meant it to be a bit of fun. If any of you were playing a bit of a prank, I wouldn't care, but please own up to it."

"I swear I never moved it," I said, and Diana shook her head.

Suzie nodded. "I didn't either, and Vicky didn't even touch it. It felt like something was pulling at it—especially at the end when it flew off the table." She shivered. "I'm going to get a bath and then I'm off to bed. After tonight, I think I'd prefer not to know what's making those strange noises. In fact, I will say it's a seagull. One with hobnailed boots."

Nervous giggles sounded from each of us as we trooped out of Suzie's room and down the stairs. "Never again," Diana said and we chorused our agreement.

Anita met us on the first floor, her eyes wide and scared in her white face. She clutched the crucifix around her neck.

"What have you all been doing up there?" she asked.

"What's the matter, Anita?" I asked. "You look scared to death." The three of us gathered around her. She backed away. Her small hands trembled and tears flowed down her pale cheeks.

"Keep away from me! You've been communing with evil. Don't try to deny it. I felt it. Here." She pointed to her head. "What have you done? What *have* you *done*?"

"It's a bit of nonsense, that's all." Diana said, reaching out a consoling hand. Anita smacked it away.

"Oh, it's far more than mere nonsense. To bring evil into our home…how could you?" She raced into her room and slammed the door.

Vicky, Diana and I stared at each other. Finally, I spoke.

"What was all that about?"

Diana shrugged. "Search me. She must have been listening at Suzie's door or something. I tell you, that girl is unhinged. She's some sort of religious maniac."

Vicky led the way into the kitchen. "Maniac or not, she's right about one thing. None of us has any explanation for what just happened up there. I'm only glad it stopped when it did." She shook her kettle at us. "Tea anyone?" Diana and I nodded. "Let's chalk it up to experience. We'll laugh about it one day."

"I hope so," I said, but something bothered me. Something I couldn't fathom yet.

Of course, as these things do, it hit me in the early hours of the morning. I knew we had broken one of Lena's cardinal rules by using the Ouija at home, but until that moment, it hadn't occurred to me we had broken a second.

We didn't say 'Goodbye'.

Chapter Three

I woke suddenly to the slamming of the front door and peered across at my clock. Six-thirty. Someone was up indecently early. By the time I dressed and bumbled my sleepy way into the kitchen, I wasn't alone. Diana leaned against her cooker, sipping a mug of tea.

"Anita's left."

That woke me up. "Left? You mean for good?"

Diana nodded. "Packed her cases and gone. I couldn't sleep and I met her coming out of the bathroom."

"What did she say?"

"Not much. Just that she couldn't wait to get out of here and we were all idiots. Or words to that effect."

"The landlord won't be pleased. No notice and presumably no one-month's rent in lieu. Should we tell him?"

"Nah, let him find out his own sweet way. I'm off to work." She poured some water in her mug and left it on the draining board.

A sound like a gentle sigh wafted through the kitchen. Diana and I stared at each other.

"Did you hear that?" I asked.

"I think it came from over there." Diana pointed at the cellar door.

"Probably the wind."

"Probably. Listen I have to go. See you tonight."

I waited a few more seconds, but the sigh did not repeat itself. Then, realizing I would be late, I hurried from the kitchen to begin my work day.

Lena had no sympathy for us. "I knew this would happen.

You're messing with things you don't understand, and now... Look, it's like leaving an open gate for a herd of cattle to pass through. Who knows what will get in?"

"But what can we do to make it right? To close that gate?"

"It may already be too late," Lena said.

I thought back to the strange sigh Diana and I had heard.

"Isn't there *anything* we can do?"

"If something has already gone through the portal you opened, it is really hard to get it to leave."

"Couldn't we hold another séance and then close it properly?"

Lena's horrified stare gave me my answer. "Definitely not. That's asking for more trouble. The only thing I can suggest is that you wait and see what happens. If nothing, you've had a lucky escape. As a precaution, I would burn or bury the cards, and do it as soon as you get home. The glass is smashed anyway, so make sure Suzie gets the remains out of the house tonight if she hasn't already. Hopefully that will stop anything else from finding its way through in the future."

"Okay, I'll do that." I wished I could get the memory of that sigh out of my head. I almost mentioned it to Lena, but decided I already looked foolish enough without making an even greater idiot out of myself.

Lena hadn't finished with me yet. "One more thing. Alice, don't ever mess with a Ouija ever again. You were the leader of that session and, if you did contact anything malevolent, it will target you. Believe me, a malevolent spirit doesn't give up on its prey. It will find you, however hard you try to escape. Open another portal and it'll be through there and onto you before you know where you are."

"Don't worry, Lena. That experience was enough. Never again."

"Promise me you'll burn those cards and get them and that smashed glass out of the house."

Two bright red spots, like overapplied blusher, flamed her normally pale cheeks.

"You're really serious about this, aren't you?" I asked, fear infecting me and making my voice wobble.

"Never more so," Lena replied. "I could tell you some real horror stories of people who have done what you did. Let's hope we're not too late to prevent you from becoming the next one."

For the rest of the day, I could think of nothing else. I wondered what was going on in that empty house, where that sigh had come from. At around fourteen years of age, I thought I saw a ghost—my grandmother, who had died a year earlier. She always wore a distinctive Lily of the Valley perfume and, one day after school, I raced up to my bedroom to change out of my school uniform. I opened my door and the scent hit me. Out of the corner of my eye, I was sure I saw a figure move. My grandmother. It passed as quickly as it had started and the smell vanished, but, for weeks afterward, I felt a warm glow whenever I thought back to that incident. Maybe she had come to say goodbye. Perhaps my imagination played tricks on me. But whatever the answer, it comforted me to believe she was still around, watching over me.

Back home that evening, I took all the cards outside into the yard and set fire to them. Suzie, brandishing a rubbish bag containing the shattered glass, watched the small conflagration as the flames burned lazily before gathering momentum. In a blaze of red and yellow, they suddenly shot up into the air and extinguished, leaving a pile of black ash.

"That's a bit weird," Suzie said.

I didn't reply. My heart pounded and I gasped for breath.

My ears pricked. "What was that?"

I had left the back door open and from inside came a mournful wailing. A cold shiver shot up my spine.

"Bloody hell!" Suzie grabbed my hand. "Who's making that noise?"

"I've no idea. Is it even human? Maybe a fox…" Even as I said it, I thought how ridiculous that sounded. For one thing, if a fox had decided to cross our threshold, we would have seen it. It would have had to brush past Suzie to get through the door.

"Come on," I said. "We can't stay out here all night." I tugged an unwilling Suzie. As I entered, the wailing stopped.

"Now that is seriously odd," I said.

"I'm sure it came from the cellar," Suzie said.

"Have you ever been down there?"

"No. I opened the door once. It was pitch black and this fusty, damp smell made me feel sick to my stomach. That was enough for me."

"What if something's trapped down there? A wounded animal or a bird?"

We crossed the floor and I realized I still gripped Suzie's hand. I let go. We stood on either side of the cellar door and listened.

I whispered to Suzie, "Can you hear anything?"

She shook her head.

The front door slammed and rapid footsteps advanced towards us.

Diana marched into the kitchen. "Whatever are you two doing?"

I put my finger to my lips. Diana came closer.

"We heard a noise. Like someone crying," Suzie whispered. "We think it came from here."

"Still nothing," I whispered, and stood back from the door. Suzie did the same. "I was worried something might have become trapped down there, but I can't hear anything now."

"Maybe whatever it is managed to escape," Diana said. "Of course, we could always go down there and investigate."

Suzie backed away. "You're not getting me down some filthy dark cellar," she said, and shuddered.

"I'd go," I said. "But I'd rather not go alone."

Diana put her ear to the door, then stood back and turned the key in the lock. It moved easily enough. She turned the handle and Suzie backed away still further.

"I don't like this one little bit," she said in a trembling voice.

"Don't be such a baby," Diana said and opened the door. Its rusty hinges creaked.

A fusty, unaired smell filled the kitchen. Diana felt around the walls. "Is there a light switch?"

"I can't remember," Suzie said. "Possibly. Yes, I think there is."

"Got it." Diana flicked the switch a few times without result.

"Damn. Bloody bulb's gone. Can't even see where it is, it's so dark in here."

"Why don't we wait until daylight and take a couple of torches with us?" I said. "Maybe we'll be able to fix the light bulb at least."

"Good idea," Diana said. She took a tentative step forward and listened. "I can't hear anything at all, so either there was nothing there in the first place or whatever you heard has made itself scarce."

"Or is lying low, waiting for its chance."

"Suzie!" I thought she was joking but her white face and tightly clasped hands spoke differently.

Terror.

"I'm going up to my room," she said. "See you in the morning."

She left us alone. I waited until I guessed she had moved out of earshot. "Is she okay?"

"I'm not sure. I think she's probably still reeling from that séance business."

"Yes, that's probably it." But doubt gnawed at me.

In fact, it would be Saturday before we plucked up the courage to tackle the cellar. What happened the next day saw us well and truly occupied for the rest of the week.

I awoke to the sound of footsteps pounding down the stairs. I looked at the clock. Six-fifteen. Grabbing my dressing gown, I wrenched my door open and almost barreled into Diana who had her hand raised ready to knock.

Vicky's door opened and she emerged—like me, tying her robe around her.

"It's Suzie," Diana said. "She's gone."

"Gone?" Vicky said. "Gone where?"

"I've no idea, but I heard this crash. It woke me up. Her room is directly above mine, so I dashed up there, to find...well, come and see for yourselves."

By now wide awake, we followed Diana back up to Suzie's flat. The door to her main room stood ajar. Inside, the chairs were knocked over, her bed was askew and unmade and the wardrobe doors were wide open.

I peered inside. "Empty." I had noticed a suitcase on top of the wardrobe on an earlier visit. It was no longer there. "Definitely looks as if she packed up and left, but why is the room in such a mess?"

Diana called from the kitchen. "She's left all her pots and pans, and it looks like she didn't take any food either. The cupboard's full."

"I don't get it," Vicky said. "Why would she up and leave without telling us?"

"She did seem quite upset last night," I said, and caught Vicky up with the previous evening's events.

"I always miss the drama," she said. "Apart from the séance, of course."

"Oh God," I said. "You don't think her leaving is linked with that, do you?"

"No," Diana said, firmly. "And I don't believe we should start getting carried away with crazy notions like that."

I nodded, trying to suppress the fear that threatened to swallow me whole. "You're right." I gazed around the room. "How about we tidy this room up so if—when—she comes back, she won't walk into a tip?"

Diana and I shoved the bed back against the wall.

"What's this?" I bent down and picked up a piece of crumpled paper, covered in symbols.

"It looks quite old," Diana said as she peered over my shoulder. "The paper's yellowed. What *are* those?"

Vicky stopped rearranging furniture and joined us. "What are you looking at?"

I showed her.

"Witch symbols. Most of them anyway. That five-pointed star within the circle is a pentacle. The square with the cross and the vertical line is a witch sign. The hexagram represents black magic. That's not good news, and the inverted pentacle with the goat's head is called the Sigil of Baphomet. That's the symbol of the Church of Satan."

That impressed me. "How do you know all this stuff?"

Vicky shrugged. "Told you. I read a lot of Dennis Wheatley

and then I started reading other stuff. Until I got scared. That's why I didn't want to go through with that séance. I wish I'd stuck to my guns and persuaded you three not to meddle with it. I've read about people driven totally insane by their experiences."

"Yes, well it's too late for that," Diana said. "We'll have to do what we can and hope Suzie decides to come back soon."

"Where do you think she got this from?" I turned the sheet over. The paper had been tightly folded into three. "She never mentioned it, so she surely can't have had it for long."

Diana took it from me and held it closer to her eyes. "There's no name on it but I'm wondering if someone slid it under her door during the night."

"None of us would do such a thing," I said.

"So that leaves Anita," Vicky said. "She could still have a key."

"Little mouse, 'I'm going to be a nun one day' Anita?" Diana laughed. "Do me a favor. You saw how she reacted when she guessed what we'd been up to. She wouldn't have any truck with this sort of thing."

"It's always the quiet ones," I said. "But you're right. I don't see her doing something like this. Not her style. Besides, she's gone. Couldn't get out of this house fast enough, so why would she return, merely to play a tasteless practical joke?"

"I think we should destroy it," Vicky said. "Burn it, just to be sure."

"It's not ours to do anything with," I said. "How about if I look after it for her? When she gets back—assuming she does—she can decide what she wants to do with it."

"As long as you don't mind having it in your room, Alice," Diana said. "I don't think I'd want it in mine."

"Me neither." Vicky shuddered.

Suddenly I wished I hadn't volunteered, but I couldn't go back on my words. I folded the paper into its original creases and tucked it in my dressing gown pocket.

I couldn't concentrate all day—a fact that my boss didn't appreciate. Three times, he pulled me up about some inaccuracy in my paperwork. Each time, he seemed more irritated than the previous occasion. I couldn't really blame him. My errors were pathetic.

Back home that evening, the remaining three of us in the house congregated in the kitchen.

"Mr. Copeland was here when I got home," Vicky said. The landlord. "I asked him about Anita and Suzie. He said Anita had been in touch, but he hadn't heard a word from Suzie and she had fallen two months in arrears with her rent. He'd called around to collect it, let himself in and found nothing. Well, we know that anyway. Good job we tidied up her room this morning. He was livid enough as it is. He said if she didn't contact him by the weekend, he would bundle up her stuff and re-let her room."

"I hadn't any idea she was in arrears," Diana said. "Did either of you? I'd have lent her the money myself if I'd known. Maybe that's why she did a moonlight flit. That piece of paper may have had nothing to do with it."

"Maybe," I said, but in my heart I didn't believe it for one second.

When I returned to my room, I took the piece of paper out of my dressing gown pocket, only to have it crumple in my hand like a dead leaf. I placed the tattered remains in my ashtray. A knock on my door. I opened it.

Vicky stood there. She wrinkled her nose. "What's that? Smells like something died."

I sniffed. A sickly, cloying aroma wafted up from the remains of the paper which gradually turned from yellow to ever-deeper shades of brown.

When I told her what it was, she became adamant. "Burn it. It's no good to Suzie in that state anyway. Burn it and be done with it." I nodded, and, as Vicky backed away, her hand covering her nose, I shut the door and grabbed a box of matches. The scraps of paper flamed quickly. I didn't expect the hissing sound that followed, as if someone had poured water on them. Dark, noxious smoke wafted up from the blackened ashtray and the brief fire died out. When the ashtray had cooled, I held it at arm's length and marched out to the garbage bin in the yard. After wrapping it in old newspaper, I dumped it in and slammed the lid on tight. I could always buy a new ashtray tomorrow.

By Saturday morning there had been no word from Suzie. Diana, Vicky, and I, armed with torches and a spare light bulb, opened the cellar door. The familiar fusty smell washed over us. Diana led the way. A flight of wooden stairs stretched before us and we carefully descended.

"There it is." Vicky shone her torch on the naked light bulb suspended from a coiled wire. "I think I can reach it if you two will provide the light."

We did so, and Vicky unscrewed the bulb. A couple of minutes later, she had the new bulb in place and went back up the stairs to switch it on.

Light flooded the stairs and we switched off our torches. Below us, a gloomy expanse awaited and we made our way down to it.

The concrete floor was filthy and littered with crumpled pages from old newspapers which had probably been used for packing years earlier. Sure enough, a couple of old tea chests came into view as we moved further into the room and needed our torches once again. We separated and moved around the dirty cellar. I picked up an ancient, rusty screwdriver, turned over a pile of worn and tattered sheets, and generally looked around for any sign of life—hoping and praying I didn't come across any cockroaches or rats.

"Can you see anything that could have made that sound you heard the other night?" Diana asked.

"Nothing, thank goodness."

"Here's something," Vicky said, and we made our way over to her. She held a piece of red cloth, and as my torch shone on it, I could see it was a dress. It looked familiar.

"Doesn't Suzie have a dress like that?" I asked.

"Exactly like this," Vicky said. "I was with her when she bought it in C & A a couple of months ago. Look, it's got their label in it. And it's her size. I'm prepared to swear this is her dress."

My palms began to sweat. "Didn't she have that on the other night?"

Diana nodded. "She did. And that was the last time any of us saw her."

No one spoke for a few moments. Then I broke the heavy silence.

"However that dress got down here, I don't believe Suzie brought it. She was terrified of this cellar."

"Nevertheless," Vicky said, brandishing the dress, "here it is. Large as life."

"Someone else must have been in this house. Maybe Mr. Copeland…"

"Why would he bring Suzie's dress down here?" Diana said. "Where did you find it, Vicky?"

"Here," she pointed to a broken coffee table. "It was lying there, folded up neatly."

"So it couldn't have been thrown from the top of the stairs?" I asked.

"Unlikely," Vicky replied. "It would have to have managed to fly through the air, take a turn to the left and land in a neat pile."

"But you said Mr. Copeland was here when you got home today," I said.

"Yes, I met him coming down the stairs. He had a face like a slapped backside."

"It doesn't make any sense," Diana said. "All he's interested in is getting his rent every month. Cash. Never checks. He's not going to bother folding up the one and only item of clothing… Hey, hang on a minute. We were in her room the day she left. Probably minutes after she'd gone. She'd taken every scrap of clothing she possessed. I'll lay odds she probably put that dress back on again and wore it when she went."

"What if she didn't leave?" I said.

"You're frightening me," Vicky said. "Are you suggesting what I think you're suggesting?"

"Well, it *is* odd, isn't it?" I said, directing my torch around the room.

Diana called out, "Suzie? Are you down here?" Her call bounced off the bare walls.

"Give me warning next time you're going to shout like that," I said. "I nearly had kittens."

"Sorry."

"I don't understand why she would come down here, take her dress off, fold it neatly and leave," I said. "None of it makes any sense."

"Agreed," Diana said. "But what if it didn't happen like that? What if someone else is involved?"

Vicky gasped. "Oh no, I'm getting out of here." She dropped the dress and ran back up the stairs, leaving Diana and me staring at each other. I stooped and picked up the discarded frock.

"I think," I said, taking a deep breath, "we had better search this place. Just in case."

I didn't need to elaborate. Diana knew exactly what I meant, and by now I truly feared the worst because I remembered something else about the morning of Suzie's disappearance. I had never heard the front or back door shut.

I blundered into an ancient standard lamp. It keeled over and smashed on the floor.

"Oh my God!" Diana said.

"Sorry," I said, stepping carefully over old paint cans and sidestepping a broken chair. Before long, I had circumnavigated the room and met up with Diana back where we had begun, at the foot of the stairs.

"We can't have missed anything," I said, offering up a silent prayer of thanks to whatever deity happened to be listening. "She isn't here."

"For which we are truly grateful," Diana said.

"Amen to that."

Back in the kitchen, I made us a coffee. "You never actually saw her that morning, did you?" I asked.

Diana shook her head. "All I heard was that crash, and that was weird because I don't understand how that could have happened when it did. Who knocked the furniture over? Surely I should have seen Suzie, or whomever, when I dashed out of my room. They would have had to fly through the window not to bump into me."

"If they went out the front or back door, they must have opened and closed it very quietly because I never heard either door, and I usually do."

"It's all very odd. All we've got is that dress. I'll hang onto it for now, if that's okay?"

"Yes," I said. "Good idea. Hopefully she'll come back for it."

"She'd better get a move on or Copeland will rent out her rooms. After all," she rolled her eyes, "the poor man needs the money."

I laughed, then a noise stopped me. A woman wailing.

"Is that what you heard before?" Diana asked.

"Yes. It's coming from the cellar. I'm sure of it."

Diana sprang forward and unlocked the cellar door.

The wailing stopped.

We waited.

Nothing.

"This is crazy," Diana said, closing the door and locking it. We paused, in case the noise would start up again. It didn't.

The scrape of a key in the front door broke the silence. The short, rotund figure of our landlord thumped his way along the hall in our direction.

"Well, have you heard from her?" His tone sounded accusing, as if we were hiding something from him. Until that moment, I hadn't really formed an opinion of the man I had only met briefly once. I did now and it wasn't favorable. I really wished I did have some information about Suzie's whereabouts, so I could keep it from him.

"Not a word," Diana said. "We're getting really worried about her."

"*You're* worried!" His face took on a reddish hue. "What about my rent? I'm not made of money. I can't afford to have rooms empty. Well, she's had her chance. I'm letting her rooms. Either of you interested?"

"Yes," I heard myself say. Diana shot me a horrified glance, but said nothing. I hadn't a clue why I had said that. It felt like a voice inside my head had suddenly woken up and taken control of me for a split second. Now it had gone again.

Mr. Copeland seemed a little taken aback. I certainly was. What could I be thinking of? He, on the other hand, didn't intend to hang around. "Right, you can move in tomorrow. I'll have her stuff bagged up and it can go in the cellar. I'll amend your rent book accordingly and let your existing room as soon as I can find someone suitable. Shouldn't take long."

The landlord apparently couldn't get out of there fast enough. Probably afraid I'd change my mind. When he had shut the door behind him, Diana turned on me.

"How could you do that? Of all the treacherous behavior!"

"Hang on a minute, Diana. Before you go off on one, think for a second." I improvised. "If, or when, Suzie comes back, she would have nowhere to stay because he's going to let her flat whether I take it or not. At least this way, she would have somewhere to live because I certainly wouldn't turn her away. My bedsit is too small for me, let alone an extra person, but I could easily fit another single bed in her room."

Diana wavered a little. "How do you know Copeland would allow it?"

"You know what sort he is. He only cares about the money. I would be responsible for that because it will be my name on the rent book."

Another key scraped in the front door. Vicky, carrying two bulging supermarket bags.

"Hi, you two, what's up? Sorry I ran out on you like that, but it really got to me down there. Did you find anything else? Any trace of Suzie apart from that dress?"

"Nothing," Diana said. "Copeland's been here. He's letting Suzie's flat. To Alice."

Vicky's mouth formed a disbelieving 'O'. "*What?*"

"Look, I'm sorry, but if Suzie comes back, she won't be homeless."

"She does have a point there," Diana said. Vicky said nothing, but the frown told me she wasn't at all convinced about my motives for this apparent betrayal. I didn't blame her. The guilt became a shroud covering me from head to foot.

It didn't let up the next day as I packed my stuff up and took it upstairs. Mr. Copeland had sent a minion armed with black plastic sacks. It took him no more than a few minutes to clear out her remaining possessions, which he duly dumped in the cellar. Then he left, without a word, even though we had instinctively formed ourselves into an impromptu guard of honor, heads bowed. As if Suzie had died, and we alone knew it.

It didn't help that I was growing increasingly uneasy. The house seemed to watch my every move. Shadows sped past me—glimpsed only at the corner of my eye. I told myself I was being paranoid, but the belief that this building possessed more than mere bricks and mortar wouldn't go away.

Diana and Vicky said little to me for the rest of the weekend and I knew the reason—they didn't know how to deal with what I had done. There's that well-worn phrase about jumping in someone's grave and I wished I could find a way of explaining my actions. I knew my words about providing a sanctuary for Suzie had fallen on largely skeptical ears. I also knew it wasn't true. Try as I might, I still couldn't explain my actions and felt every inch the traitor Diana had accused me of being.

Moving into my new flat could have been fun if the other two had thought more of me at that point. We could have had a laugh, shared a bottle of cheap wine... Instead, I went through the solitary process of packing up my few belongings and transporting them in a series of traipses up and down the stairs.

I decided to move the bed from its current position to the opposite wall where the light would be better for reading. The divan wasn't particularly heavy or awkward and I soon had it repositioned, leaving some debris behind that indicated it hadn't been moved for some considerable time.

I picked up the assorted candy wrappers and a crumpled newspaper, then stopped and stared at what lay under it—a black, slim leather-bound book. I retrieved it and read the title on the cover. *Shadows Behind the Veil. Poems by Eliza Montague Jordan.* The pages were stiff and the volume seemed quite old. Flicking through it, the poet seemed to have had a preference for the melodramatic and occasionally the downright bizarre, with overly dramatic odes to lost loves—not all of which seemed to have been human. One in particular caught my eye. Its title? "To That Which Was Lost And Now Found":

Your flaming eyes entrance me
Your body—as no other—confounds and amazes my senses.
I worship thee with my heart, and my soul I give to thee,

Unquestioning, divine, unholy, eternal…

I moved on. A poem called "The Darkest Veil" had a different quality. Dark. No love poetry here. It consisted of one verse:

Do not allow more evil to enter in this place
For it has found a home here, among the shadows of the dead
Heed my words, no devil bring, nor demon from beyond
For he already lives here and is waiting for more souls
To wait on him and serve him until His kingdom comes
At the end when all is done and those who are left may sleep,
When death's darkest veil draws over you, then shall shadows
weep.

I shivered. For some unaccountable reason, the words would stick in my mind. Especially the last line. Not that it was particularly great poetry—far from it—but there was something profoundly disturbing about its dystopian predictions. Whoever Eliza Montague Jordan had been, she appeared to have been in the grips of some kind of religious fervor.

I turned over the pages but none of the other twenty or so poems held my attention or affected me in the same way. I searched for a publisher's imprint but the book must have been self-published, probably at some not-inconsiderable cost to the author, as the binding and print quality were so fine. I could find no date of publication either.

The book suddenly felt uncomfortable in my hand and I thrust it between two of the cheap paperbacks on my newly acquired bookshelf.

Outside, evening was drawing in and the wind howled. I finished my unpacking, made myself a cup of coffee in my new kitchen, and sat down in front of the television. All around me, the house gave little creaks as the gale pounded at the roof and rattled the window.

I switched on the electric fire and settled down to watch a play, but couldn't concentrate. My attention kept wandering back to that book and that single verse kept replaying in my mind, as if it were on a continuous loop.

Suzie had never struck me as the sort to go in for poetry of any kind—least of all the sentimental or religious type. Far more likely, a previous occupant had mislaid it when they moved out.

I went to bed early that night. Tired from my exertions and relieved the fierce wind had died down, I began to drift off. From far away, I thought I heard tapping at the window. Only the rain...

Chapter Four

"Alice!"

The familiar voice broke into my dreams.

"Alice!"

I woke up. "Suzie?" I opened my eyes, as my alarm went off. The start of another working week.

I reached over and depressed the ringer. The irritating clanging stopped. I rubbed my eyes. My head felt full of cotton wool and my mouth was parched.

In the kitchen, I filled the kettle, plugged it into the wall socket and switched it on before splashing cold water over my face. It helped a little but I still felt befuddled. A mug of coffee later, my brain decided to join me in the conscious world.

Vicky was leaving as I came down the stairs. She held the door open for me, politely, returned my cheerful, "Good morning," in a grudging monotone, and we walked in awkward silence to the bus stop.

The bus was already three-quarters full and I felt a wave of relief that there would be no chance of us being able to sit together. If there had, I felt almost sure she would have sat somewhere else. The guilty shroud descended once more.

For days, I racked my brain but couldn't understand why I had grabbed the chance to rent Suzie's flat. Granted, it was much bigger and better than my old room, but when I thought of how Suzie had left, of the séance and the strange noises she had heard there, I couldn't understand why I would put myself in her position. It was hardly surprising Diana and Vicky were mad at me. If the positions were reversed, I would feel angry, too.

Every night, when I switched off my bedside lamp, I burrowed deep under the covers, fearful of hearing the slightest noise. Rain battered the window on Wednesday and I shot up in bed, my heart pounding until I realized what had caused the noise. I settled back down again, only to leap out of bed when a sudden loud gust of wind whistled and the house creaked.

My lamp stayed on that night.

Thursday night. The storm had long passed and all had become still and calm. I put down my book and switched off the lamp. I pulled the covers over my head and listened to the sound of my breathing.

A sudden noise. Scratching. At the window. I held my breath. It stopped.

I exhaled.

BANG! Something heavy landed on the roof. A sound of slithering. Something sliding down the slates.

I threw back the covers and snapped the lamp on.

I listened.

Nothing.

The seconds ticked by. Still nothing.

I debated whether I should get back in bed.

But I had to find out.

The room had grown chilly. I grabbed my dressing gown and wrapped it around me. At the window, I hesitated. If I pulled back the curtains now, what would I see? I could hear a few cars traveling up and down the main road a few yards away. Through the curtains, the amber streetlights shone as usual. I told myself it was okay. Everything would be fine. Just an empty street in the middle of the night.

I ran my dry tongue around parched lips. I took one curtain in each hand and tugged them aside.

Nothing but the neon-lit dark sky greeted me. If I opened the window, I could look up and see anything that might be hanging off the roof.

Oh yes, and supposing I *did* see something—or someone— then what would I do? I made to close the curtains.

The raven came from nowhere.

I screamed. It opened its vicious beak and gave a raucous

caw that penetrated the glass. Its vivid yellow eyes blinked at me. I screamed again and tugged the curtains closed. I backed away, clutching my chest. A lump had formed in my throat and a heavy weight pressed down on me. No one came running up the stairs. Maybe my cry hadn't been as loud as I thought.

Still the bird pecked. I willed it to stop the infernal tap, tap, tapping. I clapped my hands to my ears, threw myself onto my bed and buried myself under the covers. It didn't help. The noise of the pecking bird sounded as loud as ever.

Then it stopped, but sleep would never come that night. Although I told myself it was only a bird, it didn't help to calm me. It may have been a bird, but something didn't seem right about it.

By the end of the week, Diana and Vicky seemed to have come round a little. We were at least holding short conversations, even exchanging the odd laugh, but things weren't back to normal. It would take time for them to forgive me. They had known Suzie a lot longer than I had.

There were still only the three of us in the house.

"Has Mr. Copeland brought anyone round?" I asked as I joined Diana and Vicky in their shared kitchen.

Diana stirred a sauce. "I haven't seen anyone. He picked up the rent as usual though, so he's definitely been here."

Vicky took a sip of her tea. "He'll get new people soon enough. Two bedsits empty in the same house? Unheard of in his vocabulary."

"Still no word from Suzie," I said.

"I know," Diana said. "I wondered if we should report her as a missing person."

"Does she have any family?" I asked.

"Her mother lives in a council flat in Hunslet I think," Vicky said, but I've no idea the address. I don't even know her surname. Baxter was Suzie's married name."

"Maybe we should hang on a bit longer," I said. "I mean, apart from her dress in the cellar which, by the way, showed no signs of violence, we've nothing to go on. We can't give the police any real information, and they'll say she's a thirty-year-old mature woman capable of making her own decisions who, for some reason best known to herself, has decided to disappear."

"You've been watching too many episodes of *Z Cars*," Vicky said.

Diana finished stirring her sauce and moved the pan off the hob. "She's right, though. My uncle used to be a policeman. I can't remember how many thousand people go missing every year, but there's very little the police can do. They'll tell us that she'll come back when she's ready. It would be different if we had evidence of foul play but, as you say, the dress was clean, neatly folded and bore no trace of damage."

"So we wait then," I said.

Diana sighed. "'Fraid so. And we'd better prepare ourselves that she may never come back. We might never have the answers to our questions."

As we seemed to be getting on better, I decided to tell them about my weird experience the previous night. They listened. Diana spoke first.

"You say this bird had yellow eyes?"

"Yes. Vivid yellow."

"Definitely a raven?"

"I'm as sure as I can be. I have seen ravens before. We used to have a nesting pair in our garden."

"Ravens don't have yellow eyes. They have gray-blue ones."

"That's what was wrong. I knew there had to be something."

"How do you mean?" Vicky asked.

"It's been bothering me all day. It definitely had yellow eyes. I'm sure it was a raven and yet, you're right, Diana. The eyes were all wrong."

Vicky exchanged glances with Diana. "Shall we tell her?"

"Probably best."

"Tell me what?"

"You're not the only one who's seen that bird," Vicky said. "Suzie did, too. A few months before you moved in. Only the once as far as I'm aware, but that started it. She described what she saw exactly as you did. From the heavy thump on the roof, right through to the bird appearing from nowhere at the window. In her case, she screamed blue murder. Had the whole house up."

"I screamed. No one came."

"Sorry," Diana said. "I never heard you or I would have come up. Seriously."

Vicky stroked my arm. "I didn't either. Sorry."

"That's okay. But it's strange Suzie and I experienced the same thing. It's not an everyday occurrence, after all."

"I'd have been terrified," Vicky said. "Especially a raven. They're the subject of so much folklore. Real harbingers of doom. Or they can be."

"But *yellow* eyes?" I had no answer for that and neither did they.

A month drifted by, with no more unexplained manifestations at home. At work, my job became increasingly tedious. As a female, I was apparently deemed to be the best person to do the lion's—or should that be lioness's?—share of the filing. Although the bank liked to call itself an equal opportunity employer, in reality, the female staff had anything but parity. I suppose they felt it wasn't worth their while training us too much. After all, weren't we all destined to get married, have children and leave? My male colleagues were pretty much unanimous on that one.

At home, we had become almost resigned to Suzie's disappearance. Almost, but not quite. It still didn't add up. The timing of it, the fact she hadn't told any of us of her intentions...

Two new girls moved into the vacant bedsits and within three weeks had left to get a flat together. Mr. Copeland had vacancies once again.

I had settled into my new flat and, as I wasn't hearing any more strange noises or being startled by yellow-eyed ravens, I enjoyed having the top floor to myself, as well as the extra cupboard space.

Another week had drawn to a close. Vicky, Diana and I pretty much fully reconciled, had been out to the Yarby for a drink and the clock showed eleven-thirty when I clambered into bed and switched off my bedside lamp. I lay in the dark, thinking about nothing in particular.

Above my head, a shower of stones rattled down the roof. Hail? I switched my lamp on and sped over to the window.

Something tapped insistently on the glass. I instantly thought of the raven. I hung back and tried to make out if there was a shadow on the other side of the curtains. The tapping stopped. No sound of the bird's raucous cry. I took hold of the curtains and yanked them open. Nothing there. I peered through the window. The night appeared fine. No sign of a hailstorm, rain or anything else that could have made those noises. No one in the street below either.

After a few moments, I took a deep, calming breath, pulled the curtains shut and turned back to my bed.

A low groan echoed through the room. The floorboards creaked. Fear trickled up my back like slow-moving tendrils of ice.

I stood rigid, unable to move. My heart pounded. More stones rattled down the roof.

I heard a whimper and realized it came from me. Then a gentle whooshing sound. I squeezed my eyes shut, terrified of what I might see if I opened them.

"*Alice...*" The voice whispered to me. Unfamiliar. Male. "*Alice...*"

Something brushed my arm. My whimper became a scream. I couldn't stop.

Footsteps pounded up the stairs. Someone banged on my locked door.

"Alice! It's Diana. Let me in."

I forced my eyes open. Nothing there. I spun around. Nothing in the room.

"Alice!"

I raced to the door and wrenched it open, almost falling into Diana's arms. Vicky had joined her. I let the two of them half-carry me back into my room and sit me on the bed. With the light on, everything seemed perfectly normal.

"God, you're shaking all over." Diana rubbed my hand. "You're not cold. What on Earth happened?"

I shook my head. "Haven't a clue. I heard noises... I felt something... Someone whispered my name." How could I explain the inexplicable?

Diana and Vicky exchanged glances. "It's happening again.

Suzie experienced the same thing. It's this bloody house."

"I must have imagined it," I said. "It can't have been real."

"I doubt you did," Vicky said. "Bit too much of a coincidence that both you and Suzie should experience the same thing."

"Could that have been what drove her away? Not the arrears—or that weird piece of paper?" I asked.

"Quite possibly," Diana said. "Do you want a cup of tea or a glass of water?"

"No, I'm fine. Honestly." I didn't feel it. I don't think they believed me anyway. I pasted a smile on my face. "You both get back to bed."

I had no sleep that night and phoned in sick the next morning. Vicky and Diana checked on me before they went to work, and once the door closed, I was alone in the house, aware of every creak and shift of timbers.

By lunchtime, fed up of my own company and sick of jumping at every noise, I grabbed my purse, donned a raincoat and flat shoes and opened my door.

I got as far as the front door before a noise stopped me. From the kitchen. The sound of a woman wailing. Goose bumps rose on my arms. I turned back, took a tentative step forward, then another and another. I ran into the kitchen and, before I could stop myself, unlocked the cellar door.

The musty air hit me. Cold. Clammy.

"Suzie!" I'm not sure why I called her name.

A scream tore at my eardrums. Without thinking, I snapped the light switch on and charged down the stairs. The door slammed behind me. I spun around, suddenly aware of what I had done. I raced up the stairs again and turned the handle. It wouldn't open. Someone had locked the door from the outside.

I banged on it, yelling to be released. Nothing.

At the bottom of the stairs, a shadow moved. I clung to the banister. "Who's down there?"

This time, the shadows didn't move. The atmosphere grew darker and heavier. Once again, I banged at the door and turned the handle. Mercifully, it opened and I staggered into the kitchen. I slammed and locked the door.

The wailing began again. The sound of a tormented woman.

I clapped my hands to my ears.

"Make it stop. Make it stop." I kept repeating it like a mantra. Over and over. The wailing grew louder. It came closer. Someone coming up the stairs. Soon they would be at the top.

Almost there.

I stared at the door handle as it slowly turned. Backwards and forwards. Rattling the lock and the door. They would break through any minute.

"Please God, *no*."

The wailing and rattling stopped. I raced out of the kitchen and out the front door. No way would I return until I could be sure someone else had come home.

"I'm going to look for another flat," I told Diana and Vicky that evening. "This place has really got to me."

By their expressions, neither of them was surprised at my decision. Diana spoke first. "Why don't we rent a house together? We get on well enough."

It made sense and would probably be cheaper than our current situation. Vicky and I agreed. At the weekend, we would go through the property pages and start our search.

Knowing I wouldn't be there much longer lifted my spirits. I could breathe without feeling a crushing weight on my chest. Soon I would have a new home and, with any luck, a better job.

Diana and Vicky came to my room that evening.

"I've been to the library today," Vicky said. "I thought it might help to learn a bit about the history of this house. I found out something quite interesting."

"You're going to love this," Diana said, as she lit a cigarette.

Vicky took a notebook out of her purse and flipped a couple of sheets before she found her place. "The house itself was built in 1896, along with the others in Yarborough Drive. It was originally sold to a Josiah Underwood, formerly of Preston. He moved in, accompanied by Jessica Underwood, Martin Templar, Zechariah Short, Steven Lane, Tabitha Waterhouse, Elizabeth Jordan... the list goes on. All different surnames apart from Josiah and Jessica. All adults. Thirteen people in total."

"That must have been a tight squeeze," I said.

"Yes, but don't you get it? There were *thirteen* of them," Vicky said.

I looked blankly. Diana blew out a cloud of smoke. "That's the number you need for a witches' coven... and don't you remember, at the séance? 'We are the thirteen. We are one?'"

"There's more," Vicky said. "This group appear to have lived in this house for around five years. Then, by 1902, the inhabitants changed a bit. There were still thirteen but, apart from Josiah and Jessica Underwood, all the other names had changed."

"So eleven had moved out and eleven more had taken their place."

"I decided Josiah and Jessica might be interesting subjects to follow. Ten years later, they were still living here and there had been at least two more complete changes of co-inhabitants. Then, in 1917, the house was declared as empty."

"That would be during the First World War," I said. "Couldn't it have been bombed or something?"

"No. Just empty—and it remained that way, until Dennis Copeland bought it in 1960. It must have been derelict by then."

She had me hooked. I needed more. "Did you manage to find out what happened to Josiah and Jessica?"

"A little. I need to go back tomorrow. I only had my lunch hour. Just before I left, I did find an odd little piece in the Yorkshire Gazette dated the third of November 1909. I copied it down." She flicked over the page of her notepad and read from it. "'In court today, Mr. Josiah Underwood of Four Yarborough Drive, Chapel Allerton pleaded not guilty to crimes related to the use of witchcraft and sorcery in order to extract money fraudulently from a Miss Emma White. When asked if he was a witch, Mr. Underwood replied. "What a preposterous notion. There is no such thing." The case against him was dismissed.'"

"Well, in the immortal words of Mandy Rice-Davies, he would say that, wouldn't he?" Diana said.

"Have you seen a picture of this man?" I asked. Vicky shook her head. "I've booked tomorrow off as a day's leave so I'll try and track one down but I'm not too hopeful. I had a very helpful librarian, though, so we'll see."

Helpful she might have been, but even the diligent librarian couldn't find what apparently didn't exist. The following day, Vicky had scribbled more notes in her book and shared her results. "Something peculiar does seem to have been going on here. There were a number of complaints reported in the paper over the years. Neighbors complained about strange smells, loud chanting at all hours of the night, even men and women dancing naked around a bonfire in the back yard at midnight. Josiah Underwood was bound over in 1904 and fined for similar misdemeanors—described as 'lascivious and lewd behavior likely to cause a breach of the peace'—in 1911. I tried following the other names but, apart from Jessica, who had been charged and convicted with him, each of them seems to have dropped off the face of the planet after they moved out of here. Not that this tells us anything other than they didn't get themselves reported in the newspaper. I tried the register of deaths but, without any further information to go on, I could have been there until the middle of next year."

"Josiah and Jessica moved out around 1916 didn't they?" I said. "So where did they go?"

Vicky shrugged. "That's the most frustrating part. I can't find any record of them after that date. I kept searching until the librarian practically kicked me out, but, so far, nothing."

"So," Diana said, "are we to believe they transformed into model citizens, retired to the country and ceased dancing naked around bonfires?"

Vicky laughed. "Probably not. Maybe they got smarter and didn't get caught."

"I'll go along to the library tomorrow," I said. "See if I can pick up where you left off, Vicky. I'm not saying I'll have any more joy, but you never know."

"Good idea," Vicky said. "I'll tell you where I searched and where I intended to look next if I could have stayed longer."

"Did you discover any reason why the house should have been empty for so many years?" I asked.

"No. I don't even know whether it had been put up for sale, or left to rot until Copeland acquired it."

"Of course, if they were summoning spirits and practicing witchcraft here, it could explain some of what's been going on," Diana said. "I read somewhere that houses can retain atmosphere. That extreme evil can somehow embed itself in the bricks and mortar."

"I've read that, too," I said. "But I always dismissed it as superstitious claptrap."

"Doesn't seem quite so crazy now, does it?" Vicky said.

I agreed. Whichever way you looked at it, something wasn't right in this house. The impossible kept happening and now, whether we understood it or not, Vicky seemed to have hit on a possible cause.

I don't think I imagined the resigned look on the librarian's face when I told her what I needed. Or the weariness behind her tone.

"Someone came in here yesterday with the same request."

"That's right. I'm here to pick up where she left off. I thought I'd start with the newspaper archives. Do you have the Yorkshire Leader for 1904, 1909 and 1911?"

"On microfilm."

I smiled. "That's great."

"The full year in each instance?"

"Yes, please."

"Come with me."

I hoped and prayed the *Yorkshire Leader* could provide what the *Gazette* had so far failed to reveal—a photograph of the notorious Josiah Underwood. Being a much more sensationalist newspaper than its traditional, somewhat staid rival, I felt it would be likely to find such a character irresistible.

The librarian brought me the microfilm, showed me how to feed it into the machine and left me to it.

I wound through pages and pages of gossipy, biased reporting on anything from scandalous adulterers to womanizing vicars, and villainous bakers selling bread containing more chalk than flour. Finally my search was rewarded. In the edition of Monday September 12th, a headline grabbed my attention.

Are There Witches in Chapel Allerton?

Directly underneath, a grainy photograph showed the head and shoulders of a man with collar-length white hair. His hard stare made me shiver. I read on.

In court today, Mr. Josiah Underwood, a gentleman of independent means, residing in Yarborough Drive, Chapel Allerton, vehemently denied that he and his acquaintances had been performing rituals most commonly associated with the practice of witchcraft.

"The whole idea is preposterous," he insisted, during cross-examination.

The article went on to state that the charges had been brought by a neighbor, who claimed that the accused had sacrificed live chickens, rabbits and all manner of small animals over a number of years. He also stated, under oath, that Mr. Underwood regularly consorted in lewd behavior with his female companions, in public and without hint of shame. As no evidence of the alleged sacrifices could be produced, charges pertaining to animal cruelty were dropped, and Mr. Underwood, along with his wife, were fined and bound over to keep the peace.'

"Is it possible to have a photostat of this page?" I asked the librarian.

"There'll be a charge, I'm afraid."

"That's okay," I said, hoping I had enough cash on me. I showed her the page I wanted.

My later searches produced nothing of any value. Each time Underwood appeared in court, the *Leader* reproduced the same photograph and I learned nothing new. Before I knew it, two hours had flown by.

"We close at one p.m. on Saturdays," the librarian said. I checked the clock. Ten minutes left. No time to start on any new research. I thanked her, handed over the required fee, took my photocopy and left.

Back home, Vicky and Diana cast their eyes over the article and the photograph.

"He's an evil-looking sod," Diana said.

"It's those eyes," Vicky said. "They're creepy. It's as if he can really see you looking at him."

"Reminds me of Rasputin," I said. "There's a famous photograph of him where he has his arm raised as if he's giving a blessing. He had the same kind of eyes. Piercing. Searching. Like they could see into your soul."

Vicky put her hand up. "Stop. You're giving me goose bumps."

"Sorry."

"No, she's right," Diana said. "I know the picture you mean. Gave me the chills the first time I saw it. This Josiah Underwood does have that same intense stare."

I looked at the photograph again and the hairs on the back of my neck prickled. Something felt alarmingly familiar about him. That gaze. A flash of memory—the raven. No, crazy thoughts. Suddenly I didn't want to hold it anymore. The paper had become moist and clammy in my hand. Unpleasant to touch. I folded it and tucked it behind the clock on my mantelpiece.

I have no idea what woke me in the middle of the night, but my heart thumped and I had broken out in a sweat. I lay still in the darkness and listened, but all remained quiet. I couldn't see my clock in the dark and felt too scared to switch on the light.

Across the room, a white mist began to form. I held my breath until my lungs felt as if they would burst if I kept it in any longer. Slowly, and I hoped silently, I exhaled.

The mist swirled. I prayed it wouldn't come any closer but gradually it drifted nearer. A strong smell of rotten eggs wafted with it. I shrank to the edge of my bed, until I could retreat no further. I leaned against the wall, hunched up, my knees under my chin, as small as I could become.

Still, the mist advanced, agonizingly slow. Soon it would be on me. I wanted to cry for help, but my mouth wouldn't open. My jaw locked, my muscles froze.

The mist changed shape. It started to take form. Human form. Tall, male. That's all I could make out.

"Alice...Alice..." The voice had an almost hypnotic quality.

My jaw unlocked. "Get away from me. What do you want?"

That laugh. I had heard it before. The mist lost its form and swirled away. I continued to stare long after it had vanished. I didn't trust what I believed I had seen. I must have dreamed it.

Eventually I fell asleep and woke feeling more tired than when I had gone to bed. I dragged myself up and crossed the chilly room to turn on the electric fire. Hopefully I had put enough money in the meter to keep it going for a few hours. The clock on the mantelpiece showed twenty minutes past ten. I stared at it for a moment while my befuddled brain kicked in. Something was missing. Then I realized the photostat of Underwood's trial had disappeared.

Chapter Five

Vicky waved a piece of paper around. "It's from Mr. Copeland. Apparently he's gone on holiday for a couple of weeks and asks us if we would show any prospective new tenants round."

"He's left the keys to the vacant rooms?" That seemed a bit too trusting for him.

"Oh no. We are to show them *our* rooms and explain that the empty ones are just like them."

"Typical!" Diana flung a wet tea towel onto the draining board. "That means I'll have to keep my room clean and tidy. Can't have people thinking I'm a slut."

Vicky and I laughed. "Never mind, Diana," Vicky said. "Think of all those missing pairs of knickers you'll find when you get to the bottom of that pile of clothes on your chair."

Diana grimaced.

"At least we'll be able to vet the new lot. Make sure we don't get any odd people," I said. "Not that we're likely to be here long enough for it to matter."

"I don't know. It could take a while to find somewhere we like," Vicky said. "Given that we're all on a pretty tight budget."

"We'll find somewhere," Diana said. "I have every confidence in us."

We all heard it at the same time. A deep sigh that seemed to come from nowhere and everywhere at once.

"Let's get out of here," Diana said, already half way down the hall. We didn't need to be told twice.

Outside in the cool autumn air, we breathed easier.

"Did that really happen?" Vicky asked.

"We have to get out of that house," Diana said.

I agreed, but a nagging, irrational doubt in the pit of my stomach wouldn't leave me alone. Would the house let us go?

Almost a week passed and no one came to look at the rooms. Finally, on Thursday evening, I opened the door to a smartly dressed woman on the doorstep.

"I'm Roisin Devlin. I've come about the room." Her voice matched her appearance. A pretty, smiling face, olive complexion and a lilting Irish brogue.

I opened the door wider. "I'm Alice Lorrimer. Come in." She did, but a change came over her the instant she stepped over the threshold. The smile disappeared. She clutched a small crucifix at her throat while I prayed we weren't in for another religious fanatic.

I led her upstairs, noting she seemed a little unwilling to follow me.

"I'm sorry we don't have keys to the spare rooms but there's one on the ground floor at the back and the other one is here." I pointed at the door of number four. "Mine is the only one with its own kitchen. I'm on the top floor and you're welcome to come up for a cup of tea. I'll try and answer any questions you may have."

She didn't say a word and I was struck by how pale she had become. She followed me up the final flight of stairs but stopped halfway.

"Whatever's the matter?" I asked.

"I'm sorry. I…" She turned around and started down the stairs a good deal faster than she had mounted them. I followed her.

"Are you okay?" I asked.

"I will be when I get out of this house," she said. "How can you live there with…*that?*"

She flung open the front door so hard it banged against the wall. The house shook. She had already made it halfway down the path when I called out to her.

"What do you mean? What are we living with?"

I have never seen a more pitying gaze. "Abomination. It's all around you. Don't you *feel* it?" She crossed herself rapidly and clutched at the crucifix again. Then she had gone, as fast as her high heels would allow, leaving me once again perplexed and anxious.

When I told Vicky and Diana about it, Vicky spoke my thoughts. "The sooner we get out of this house the better."

I awoke in the darkness. Outside, rain beat on the window. I closed my eyes and turned over, pulling the covers more tightly around me as the chill penetrated my nightdress. I faced into the room. A noise. A whooshing sound as if someone had shaken a sheet. My eyes snapped open. A shaft of moonlight shone through the thin curtains, casting an eerie glow over the far end of the room. In that glow, something moved. My breath caught in my throat. I watched the shape unfurl, grow, take human form. I gripped the covers hard. The moonlight faded and disappeared—and with it, the shape. I don't know how long I stared into the darkness. Nothing moved. A wave of extreme weariness washed over me and I drifted back into a troubled sleep.

"A friend of mine at work told me about a house on her road today," Diana said the following evening. "It's in Roundhay. If it's anything like hers, it could be exactly what we're looking for."

I inhaled and crossed my fingers. "Oh God, I hope so."

The next evening, the three of us sat in Vicky's room and split a bottle of chilled white wine between us while we quizzed Diana about the house she had been to see.

"What was it like?" I asked.

"Big enough. On a good bus route into town and it's been looked after. Even the decorations are recent and someone has actually thought about the color scheme. The kitchen is modern and fully fitted. New gas stove. Central heating, too. I really like it and the rent is within our price range. An estate agent is administering it on behalf of the owner and, basically, if you both agree with me, we can have it, subject to satisfactory references."

"When can we go and see it?" Vicky asked.

"Monday evening after work. I don't think you'll be disappointed."

"Just get us out of here!" I said.

"I'll drink to that," Vicky clinked her glass with mine and then Diana's. "Here's to our probable new home." We raised our glasses, as the house shuddered.

"What the *hell*?" In my haste to stand up, I spilled my wine.

The echoing sigh sent shivers through my body. I tasted bile and swallowed hard. I guessed my face had turned as white as Diana's and Vicky's.

"Oh my God," Vicky clapped her hand over her mouth. I followed her terrified gaze.

In the center of the room, a dense, gray mist formed, from the floor upward. Shapes moved around within it. As they took more solid form, voices sang, faintly at first, then louder.

"They're *chanting*," I said. I couldn't make out the words. They seemed to be in another language.

"There's so many of them," Vicky said. "Who are they? What do they want?"

The mist swirled and then dissipated. Thirteen men and women, dressed in Edwardian dark gray, yet oddly transparent, stood in a circle, ignoring us. Their chants grew louder. I tried to move, but my feet wouldn't budge.

"Can anyone get to the door?" I asked. Still the group ignored us.

"No," Vicky and Diana replied.

A tall, thin man with long white hair moved to the center of the circle. He held a live—yet ghostly—chicken in one hand. It flapped and clucked. A glint of metal in his other hand revealed a sharp, evil-looking dagger.

Vicky screamed as he slit the chicken's throat. Blood poured from the still-flapping bird, but disappeared before it hit the floor.

The man stared at us. He, at least, seemed aware of our existence. The cold, steely eyes invaded my mind and planted unwanted images. A bonfire. Thirteen men and women dancing around it, naked, chanting. A young woman, also naked, except for the gag and ropes binding her to a wooden post. The man with white hair held a sword in his hand. He raised his arms high and wide. The sound of screaming. A roar. Louder than any animal. In the flickering light cast by the bonfire against the blackness of night, a horned figure, eight feet tall, loomed. Its eyes flamed red and its scaly skin shone with iridescent green. Its eyes met mine and I filled with hopelessness and despair. The vision vanished. I felt a painful tug as the thoughts were forcibly dragged from my mind. What the man had put there, he took away, with no pity for the hurt he inflicted. I staggered forward, clutching my head.

"They've gone," Diana said.

I opened my eyes. We were alone once more. No sign anyone else had ever been there. A sudden movement grabbed my attention.

"The wall! It's *moving*." I glanced back at Vicky, and then at Diana who stood with her mouth slightly open. "It can't *do* that."

Strange undulations produced a ripple effect along the wall.

Diana grabbed my hand. "It's...*breathing*."

The ripples became more regular, seeming as if that wall inhaled and exhaled. Its entire length rose and fell rhythmically. With every movement, a scraping sound as that of bricks rubbing together, punctured the silence in the room.

"I can't stay here another night." Diana's voice quaked. "I'm going to grab some things and go to a B and B."

"I'll join you," I said.

"Me, too." Vicky stepped back to retrieve a suitcase from the top of her wardrobe.

She didn't get there.

The wall creaked and expanded. Further along, the door buckled, then fell off its hinges, clattering to the floor as the wall filled the space and closed up.

The three of us clung together.

"The window!" Vicky wrenched herself free of our grasp and raced over to try and open it. "We can get out of here." She tugged at the catch. "The bloody thing's stuck. I can't get it unlatched."

"Smash it!" Diana said, picking up a dining chair and hoisting it above her head.

Vicky let out a scream and clutched her hand. "It...I don't believe that happened."

"What?" I pulled her out of the way as Diana rushed forward, tossing the chair at the window. We all ducked to avoid the inevitable shards of glass. To our right, the wall heaved and expanded again.

The glass didn't shatter. The chair smashed on the floor as if it had been caught and thrown back.

Vicky's voice trembled. "I saw a hand...long nails. It *scratched* me."

Her damaged hand poured blood. It didn't make sense, but the bleeding scrapes did resemble scratches, as if someone had raked their nails across the back of her hand. I grabbed a silk scarf off a chair and bound the wound as tightly as I could. Vicky sobbed as Diana stared at the ruined chair.

"Please tell me I'm going to wake up in a minute," she said.

Under our feet, the floor shook. Above us, the lampshade covering the main light swayed erratically.

"We're never going to get out of here, are we?" Vicky said, her reddened eyes looking at me. I wanted to reassure her, but could think of nothing to say.

The tremors under our feet had grown much stronger. The carpet lifted and fell. Beneath it, the floorboards creaked. Sounds of splintering all around us.

Diana gave a cry. "What's happening?"

I had no more idea than she had. We clung together, tears flowing freely, as slowly the walls closed in and we sank down into darkness.

Chapter Six
2019

The invitation came on white card, and because its arrival was so unexpected, I read it three times before I believed my eyes.

Dear Alice. I hope you are well. It's been so many years since we all lived together at 4 Yarborough Drive and I thought it was high time we met up there for a reunion. I'm sure lots has happened to you this past 47 years and it will be great to catch up. I thought Saturday July 20th at around 3p.m would be a good time. Incidentally, did you know they're demolishing all the houses on that side of the road? The bull-dozers move in on Monday 22nd. They're building some new houses apparently. Hope you can make it on Saturday. Love, Suzie.

When I had recovered, I made a cup of coffee and re-read the card a few more times. A hundred questions flooded my mind. What had happened to Suzie all those years ago? How had she found me? Had she traced the others? I'd lost touch with Vicky and Diana years earlier. I couldn't even remember when. In fact, so much of that time remained a complete blur. I searched my brain for answers and none came.

How could I not go on Saturday?

Eventually, I stood up from the chair I had sat in for a shade too long. I straightened my stiff back and wandered across to the over-filled bookcase. I rummaged among the paperbacks, most of which had been there for as long as I could remember.

Some I still hadn't read. Jackie Collins, James Herbert, Victoria Holt… And I couldn't remember a word of any of them. Old age creeping up on me, I suppose.

My fingers touched a slim volume of poetry. Strange because I couldn't remember seeing it since I left Yarborough Drive, where I could have sworn I left it. I pulled it out, dislodging a couple of Agatha Christie mysteries along the way. The book fell open and the all-too-familiar line of that poem I had first read all those years ago grabbed my attention:

When death's darkest veil draws over you, then shall shadows weep.

For some reason now, it seemed to hold more meaning than ever. Although what that meaning was, I had no idea.

Time hadn't been especially kind to Yarborough Drive. The pub still stood there and the houses on one side looked relatively well cared for, but on the side where I had lived, windows were broken, gates off their hinges, paint flaked and peeling, and window frames looked gray and rotten. A sign showing a smiling, youthful retired couple informed me that a new retirement complex of apartments and bungalows would be ready the following spring. As none of the existing properties had been demolished yet, I rather doubted it.

Some shattered slates littered the short path leading to the front door of number four and, judging by the quantity of them, the roof had to be leaking.

I tried the door handle. To my surprise, it turned and the door reluctantly opened, creaking badly as the warped wood scraped along the tiled floor. I took a tentative step inside. A familiar damp, fusty smell greeted me—the smell I associated with the cellar.

"Hello?" My voice echoed as it bounced off the bare walls. I listened. Nothing. I moved further inside, taking care to avoid tripping over broken bits of furniture which looked like someone had taken a sledgehammer to them. Impossible to tell what had once been a chair or an occasional table, although some shattered timbers reminded me a little of Vicky's wardrobe. I tried what had been her door. The last time I had seen it had

surely been our last day in the house. It had lain on her floor…
If only I could remember….

I turned the handle. Locked. Or jammed.

I moved along the hall, ignoring the next door. My first
room in this house had been empty when I was last here. In the
communal kitchen, doors hung off cookers, the large cupboard
stood open, any remaining bottles long since pilfered. I smiled,
remembering our trips down to the Yarby.

Inevitably, my gaze alighted on the cellar door. Shut. But
locked? I tried to open it and got my answer. I couldn't see the
key anywhere. Probably as well.

A noise from the hall made me jump. A woman I gauged to
be in her late sixties joined me in the kitchen.

"Alice Lorrimer, as I live and breathe, it *is* you." She smiled
and I saw past the gray hair.

"Diana!" We embraced. "How have you been?"

"I've been well. And happy. I've been happy. How about
you?"

We stood back, still holding hands. "I can't complain," I
said. "It's so good to see you after all these years."

"Too many years." Diana raised her eyes skyward. "How
did we manage to lose touch? I can't even remember when."

"Me neither. One of those things. You get busy with life.
Other priorities take over. So, what did you make of Suzie's
invitation? I was gobsmacked."

"Me, too. I don't suppose you ever heard from her down the
years either?"

I shook my head.

"I don't even know how she got my address," Diana said.

"Internet, I expect. She probably searched the electoral roll
or something."

"She did a thorough job of it then. I changed my name
twice."

"You married then?"

"Once widowed and once divorced. Happily single these
days. How about you?"

"Only the one marriage and divorce," I said. "Changed my
name back, so I would have been easier for her to find."

"I wonder if Vicky will make it."

A voice rang out along the hall. "She will and she's here."

No mistaking that red hair, although I suspected that these days it had a little help. Vicky threw her arms around each of us in turn.

"Well this is a turn-up, isn't it?" she said. "And the old place is looking a right dump. It's half-demolished already."

"Sad, really," I said, looking around at the filthy kitchen where, in addition to the damp fustiness, a sour stench of dirty drains wrinkled my nostrils. "It doesn't seem nearly so frightening now."

We lapsed into a companionable silence. Like me, I imagined my two old friends were probably casting their minds back all those years.

"Did you ever work out what happened?" I asked.

Diana and Vicky both shook their heads.

"I put it out of my mind," Vicky said. "I can't remember the last time I ever thought about it. And now, when I try, there are gaps in my memory. Do you find that, too?"

I nodded, and Diana spoke, echoing my own thoughts. "It's as if my brain has decided it's not good for me to remember and has thrown away those particular memories. Or put them firmly under lock and key. Self-preservation."

"I nearly didn't come," Vicky said. "I'm still not at all sure it's a good idea to rake up the past like that, but in the end, I had to. I have to find out what happened to Suzie. Is she here?"

"Not as far as I can tell," I said. "But I haven't ventured upstairs yet. I'm not even sure it's safe to do so."

"I'm guessing neither of you have been down there yet," Vicky pointed at the cellar door.

"No," I said. "And I don't intend to either. Besides, the key's missing."

The room darkened. We drew closer together, as if by instinct. A joint need for protection.

"What the hell?" I followed Vicky's gaze to the window. Either the sky had suddenly grown blacker or something masked the glass. The words of that poem "The Darkest Veil" flashed into my mind.

"'When death's darkest veil draws over you, then shall shadows weep.'"

"What?" Only when Diana spoke did I realize I had uttered the words out loud.

"Oh, nothing. A daft poem by someone called Eliza Montague Jordan."

"The name sounds familiar," Vicky said.

"Look, it's getting brighter. Must have been a black cloud. There wasn't an eclipse due today, was there?"

"I don't think so," Vicky said. "Come on, let's go upstairs. I've had enough of this room."

Vicky led the way as we stepped over old newspapers, fallen plaster, peeled paint and torn wallpaper littering the stairs. On the first floor, the doors were mostly off their hinges. We carried on up to my old flat. It too had been wrecked, furniture smashed and overturned, the same old mattress—now with protruding rusty springs and unmentionable stains.

"Someone's been dossing here," Diana said as she kicked a couple of empty beer cans across the floor of her old room.

Something in the corner of the room caught my eye. I strolled over to it and bent down. "Hypodermic," I said.

"Druggies." Diana wrinkled her nose.

"I wish Suzie would get here." Diana hugged herself. "This place is starting to get to me."

"And me," I replied, shivering.

"Well, aren't you all a sight for sore eyes?"

We turned as one. Suzie stood in the doorway, a broad grin lighting up her face.

We rushed towards her and embraced in a group hug. When we finally separated, I said, "You look amazing. I swear you haven't aged a day since I last saw you." The same blonde, pixie bob, shining eyes, clear skin. She must have had some surgical help, of the very best kind.

Suzie laughed. "You all look great, too. I've missed you."

"But, what happened to you?" Vicky spoke for us all.

Suzie tapped the side of her nose with her forefinger. "Tell you later. Right now, you need to come with me."

We followed her back down the stairs and stopped outside

Vicky's room. I felt an unpleasant prickling along my arms.

Suzie produced a key and inserted it in the lock.

We all hung back. Half-remembered scenes from that long-ago day played through my mind like some sort of bizarre film trailer. The picture was incomplete, as if it had happened to someone else and I was trying to access their brain for the missing pieces. I guessed Vicky and Diana felt the same.

Suzie opened the door. "Come on then," she said.

Diana, Vicky and I exchanged nervous glances. I wondered if they remembered more than me. The biggest shock came when we crossed out of the hall.

Vicky gazed around the room. "It's the same."

My last hazy memory of this room had been the scene of devastation it had become on that terrible day. Someone had gone to a great deal of trouble to restore it to precisely the same as it had looked when Vicky lived here—even down to matching the flowery wallpaper.

"It's immaculate," I said. "But how can it be in this condition when the rest of the house is falling down and about to be demolished anyway?"

Again Suzie made that nose-tapping gesture. It began to annoy me.

"All in good time. Let's sit down and catch up, shall we?"

Why did I feel so strongly that she had so many more answers than the rest of us? Not only about herself, but about this house and everything that had happened in it?

I sat next to Diana on the settee. Vicky lowered herself into an armchair under the window. Suzie remained standing.

"I know you've all got loads of questions," she said. "And I promise I will try and answer them all for you, but you need to bear with me. First I want you to tell me what you have all been getting up to. Diana, would you like to start?"

Diana blinked a couple of times. "I got married, divorced my first husband two years later, and married the next man that asked me. No children. I quit my job some years back and live in a small flat in Huddersfield."

"What was your first husband like? What was his name?"

Strange questions, I thought, but we all knew Suzie could be unpredictable. Diana stared at her, as if she couldn't remember the answers.

"Don…no…John. I haven't thought about him in years. He was okay I suppose. Not a lot to say about him really."

Suzie nodded and turned to me. I noticed Diana breathe a quick sigh of relief. Now, my turn under the spotlight.

"I've been married and divorced once and still live in the house we bought together. I worked for the bank until last year. Like Diana, I had no children."

"And you've been happy? Got some great memories?"

"Yes." Why wouldn't I? Not that I could recall any specific examples at that moment. Age again.

Suzie smiled.

Vicky told a similar story to the rest of us, only in her case she did have a child. Sadly he died at a few days old. The rest of her life to date had been spent working in the civil service until, like me, she retired last year.

"Your turn, Suzie," I said. "What happened to you all those years ago? Why did you leave? Where did you go?"

Suzie's smile grated on me. She seemed so smug. Not at all like the old Suzie, even if she didn't look as if she had aged a day.

"Oh my story's quite simple," she said. "I never left here."

Chapter Seven

The silence seemed to last for hours, although in reality, it couldn't have been more than a couple of minutes before Diana gave voice to my thoughts as well as hers and, no doubt, Vicky's.

"What do you mean, you never left here? You walked out one morning forty-seven years ago and none of us has seen or heard of you since. Until we received those invitations."

Still that infuriating smile. "I have been here the whole time. You simply weren't aware of me."

Diana's face reddened. "Suzie, that's plain crazy. Do you think we're all stupid? Come on, where have you been really?"

The smile vanished. "I've been *here* the entire time."

"Oh yes?" Diana's voice rose. "Where? In the walls? Under the floorboards? Down in the cellar? No, you couldn't have been there because we came looking for you and all we found was your red dress."

"I know," Suzie said. "I saw you."

"But you weren't *there*. Oh someone else please take over, I'm getting nowhere."

I decided to give it a go. "Why don't you start at the beginning and tell us what happened, Suzie. Start from that morning when, as far as we were all concerned, you left."

Suzie blinked a couple of times. "Very well. You all know there is something different about this house. The tapping at the window, the footsteps on the roof and then, most significantly for all of you, the experience you had in this room that day."

"Yes, we're aware of that," Diana said.

Suzie shot her a quick glare. "I know Vicky did her

homework and discovered the house had once belonged to Josiah Underwood and his coven."

"So they were witches then?" I asked.

Suzie nodded. "They simply called themselves The Thirteen. An odd and fluid collection of artists, writers, tradesmen, widows and spinsters. Josiah and his wife were the only couple. As members left they were always replaced. Then war came and it became harder to maintain the thirteen as all the young men were being conscripted. Josiah had to find another way."

"And another house presumably," I said. I caught Vicky's eye. "Didn't you say the house was listed as uninhabited in 1917?"

"I think so," she said. "Definitely around that time."

"This house is never empty," Suzie said. "There are people all around you, right now. Listening. Watching."

I shuddered. Diana spun round. "There's no one here but us," she said, "Oh cut the bullshit, Suzie. Tell us the truth."

"She is telling the truth," I heard myself say, though how I could possibly know this I hadn't a clue, except... "Can't you feel it?" I rubbed my icy hands together. Something stroked my hair. I jerked forward and Suzie laughed.

"Now do you believe me?" she said.

Diana gasped. "Something grabbed my arm."

Vicky screamed. "Get *off* me! God, something's leaning on my shoulder." She grabbed hold of my arm. "Suzie, what the *hell* is going on here?"

"I'll let you work that out for yourselves in due course," she said and I wanted to shake her, to drag the information out of her in whatever way I could.

"Suzie," Diana said. "This has gone far enough. Please stop whatever you're doing to us right now and answer our questions honestly."

We were treated to the smug smile as well as wide-eyed innocence this time. "I have not uttered one lie since you arrived. But, as you are all having so much trouble accepting what I am telling you, let's delve a little deeper into your lives. Alice. Let's start with you. Tell us everything you can remember about your life since that day in Vicky's room."

I searched my mind. "I told you. I got married, worked at the bank—"

"No, no. I don't mean generalizations. Tell us what happened straight after that phenomenon frightened you all."

I stared at her. I struggled to recall anything. I had been married—but, if so, who was he? Only a shadowy, faceless presence came into my mind, as if captured in a dream. I had worked for the bank all those years, but couldn't fathom why on earth I would have stayed there, knowing how much I had grown to hate it. As for my last role there, nothing surfaced. It seemed lost in fog, along with the rest of my life. I struggled to recall my mother and father. I could only remember them as they would have been in 1972. What had become of them? My mind drew a complete blank. "I don't remember," I said. "I seem to have blocked it out. The last thing I can recall from that day is this big hole opening in the floor."

"And the next thing you remember?"

Again my mind performed a fruitless search. "It's all a bit hazy. I went on with my life I suppose."

"And you three never got that house together?"

"How did you find out about that?" Diana asked.

"I told you, I never left here. Of course I knew about it."

I exchanged confused glances with Vicky and Diana. My heart thumped painfully and I had the sensation of rushing water in my ears. "Did we?" I asked. "I can't believe I can't remember."

"I can't either." Vicky said. "I don't think we did, but I have no idea why we wouldn't. We had first refusal on that house Diana had seen. It sounded ideal."

"It was," she said. "For the record, I can't remember either." She sighed. "I want to get out of here now. It's becoming too oppressive."

I knew what she meant. The atmosphere felt heavy and, inexplicably, the room felt crowded. "I'll join you," I said.

"Let's go over to the Yarby," Vicky said.

"Oh no. I don't think so." Suzie's tone unnerved me. She had issued an order, and I, for one, didn't think it would be wise to disobey.

"And why not?" Diana demanded.

"Because our business here isn't finished. It's nowhere near finished."

Something about her tone chilled my blood. This wasn't the Suzie I remembered, but at this moment, I could barely remember a single detail of my life since 1972, so how could I even trust what memories I had? I shivered. The room had grown icy and its heavy atmosphere bore down on me with almost physical weight.

"What's happening here?" I asked. "Does anyone else feel like they're being crushed?"

Vicky and Diana nodded. Suzie remained impassive. The smug smile had gone, replaced with a cold, hard stare. As I looked into those brown eyes, I flinched. Instead of the genuine warmth and humor I associated with her, I saw emptiness. The old Suzie had gone. The new Suzie—an imposter.

"Who are you really?" The words were out before I could check myself. "You can't be Suzie, so who are you?"

"You couldn't be more wrong. *I* am Suzie, just as *you* are Alice."

"This is ridiculous," Diana said, as she turned towards the door. "I'm leaving. Anyone joining me?"

Suzie barred her way. "That won't be happening. You are all staying here."

Diana made to push her out of the way, but Suzie ducked. Diana fell backwards and crashed to the floor. Vicky and I rushed to help her.

My temper exploded at Suzie. "What the *hell* did you do that for?"

Suzie rewarded my fury with that smug smile. "Me? I did nothing. Did I, Diana?"

Vicky and I each took one of Diana's arms and helped her to her feet. She seemed more stunned than physically injured.

"She's right," Diana said, her breath coming in short gasps. "She never touched me. Something... I don't know what... Something punched my stomach and pushed me back."

"We're definitely getting out of here," Vicky said. "Come on." The three of us darted forward. Something grabbed my shoulders and dragged me back. Invisible hands held my arms in a bruising grip. Vicky and Diana struggled, as did I.

Suzie laughed—a horrible, mocking sound. "You might as well accept that you are going nowhere. He won't let you. *They* won't let you. Here you are and here you will stay."

I stopped struggling. Her words held such a note of finality, but Diana wouldn't give up.

"I don't know how you're doing this, Suzie, but it has to stop. *Now.*"

"Me? I'm doing nothing. And struggling like that will only make him more determined."

From far away, came a rushing sound like a mighty gale. Moving closer. My hair blew around my face, the force nearly knocked me off my feet and I staggered against the invisible hands that still clung to my arms.

Beside me, Vicky sobbed. "Make it stop, Suzie. For God's sake make it stop."

"God?" Suzie laughed. "No, God doesn't come into it."

"For pity's sake then," Diana shouted over the roar of the wind.

A sudden dark mist robbed me of sight. All I could sense was a swirling mass. All I could feel were the hands gripping me and the wind buffeting my face and body. A strong smell of sulfur filled the air and we coughed and spluttered as it choked us.

In the mist I began to make out shapes. Human figures. A hag's face. Its skull features barely covered with peeling skin. Dark green. Almost black. It bared its rotten teeth and hissed— then vanished. A man's face. Familiar. Jutting, pointed chin, penetrating gray eyes, flecked with yellow, shoulder-length white hair. Josiah Underwood emerged from the mist, shadowy and ethereal at first, then growing clearer, more solid, as the wind died down and the mist evaporated. He stared at us, his eyes holding a menace so black and soul-less that I feared for us all in that moment.

Behind him, swirling shapes transformed into nine men and women. Most hung back, content to stare at us with those same eyes as their master's. Because of that there could be no doubt. Josiah Underwood controlled everything that went on in this room. Including Suzie.

One woman, in Edwardian dress, stepped forward and stood next to her leader.

"Elizabeth Jordan," Suzie said. "Only you, Alice, know her better as Eliza Montague Jordan."

"'The Darkest Veil.'" My voice was no more than a whisper. The woman nodded but didn't speak.

"That's right," Suzie said. "She gained all her inspiration from here. From her master."

Another woman stepped forward and took the man's arm.

"Jessica Underwood," Suzie said. "And now we are thirteen."

Chapter Eight
1976

Sister Immaculata, formerly known as Anita Lewis, adjusted her wimple. No mirrors were allowed in the convent, nor untidiness of dress or person, so the nun felt around her head and shoulders, ensuring she would be properly attired when she opened the door of her cell.

She clutched the simple wooden cross around her neck and breathed deeply. She closed her eyes.

Hail Mary, Full of Grace, The Lord is with thee. Blessed art thou among women, and blessed is the fruit of thy womb, Jesus. Holy Mary, Mother of God, pray for us sinners now, and at the hour of our death. Amen.

She repeated the silent prayer ten times and followed it with an "Our Father". Calmer, she opened her eyes and let go of the cross. Today was a big day. Finally, the Mother Superior was allowing her to go back to Yarborough Drive. But not alone, and for that Sister Immaculata felt grateful. Father Patrick Shaughnessy would go with her. The elderly priest had some experience in casting out demons—and in debunking fakes.

Reverend Mother had prayed on her decision for weeks before she called the nun into her office.

"Sister, you will soon be taking your vows and I know this matter has troubled you for some years."

"Yes, Reverend Mother. Ever since I fled from that cursed house, I have feared for the fate of the girls I left behind. They invited evil in, but I don't believe they intended to." Sister

Immaculata stared down at her clasped hands. She always found the Reverend Mother's intense gaze disturbing.

"After many hours of prayer and contemplation, I am driven to grant your request. Father Patrick will accompany you and you are to obey his requests. He knows how to keep both of you safe from whatever may remain in that house. Will you promise me that you will do as he tells you?"

Sister Immaculata forced herself to meet the clear blue eyes of the Mother Superior. "Yes, Reverend Mother. I promise."

"Then you shall go tomorrow afternoon. Now we will pray together for your safety and, if necessary, success."

At just after three the following afternoon, Sister Immaculata stared up at the ruined house. Beside her, Father Patrick fingered his rosary and tutted.

"You're sure this is the right place, Sister?" he asked. "It looks as if no one has lived in it for years. All those boarded-up windows. Dear me." He sighed.

"This is definitely where I lived. Number four. I had the bedsit at the back on the first floor." Sister Immaculata's voice wavered. "I told them they shouldn't have done it. I knew no good would come of it."

"The Reverend Mother told me that, all through your novitiate, you have begged to be allowed back here. You said it weighed on your mind."

"I have felt more and more I did the wrong thing. I shouldn't have deserted those girls. They had no idea what they had done. At least I knew the danger they were putting us all in. I should have stayed and help them fight it. I should have gone to the priest of my local church and told him so he could bless the house before any more damage could be done. Now look at the place." She made a sweeping gesture with her arm. "You can practically taste the evil inside from here."

Father Patrick frowned. "Sister, you have an acute sense of the spiritual and that is to be commended, but please don't confuse that with a lively imagination. There are a hundred and more reasons why this building has been left to rot like this."

Sister Immaculata stared at him. Surely Father Patrick must

sense the darkness. She could taste the rot and smell the fetid atmosphere that would be magnified a hundredfold when they opened the door. "Father, how can I explain this? The night the four of them held that séance, I was sitting in my room in quiet meditation. My eye became drawn to the corner of the room and I saw a vision. An angel crying. Not real and solid as you and I are, but ghostly. I should have been afraid but I wasn't. As I continued to watch, a voice came into my mind. It told me evil had entered through a portal in the house. Then the vision faded and left me with so many questions. I heard a crash from upstairs and I jumped out of my chair and out of my room. Presently three of the girls came down and I confronted them, but they didn't understand. They thought I was mad. Some kind of religious freak. The next day, I left, and the torment has grown within me until I know I cannot take my vows until I have put right what I failed to put right four years ago."

Father Patrick listened intently. When she had finished, he nodded and sighed. "I must warn you, Sister, I have seen many strange things over the years. I have witnessed heavy furniture moving all by itself. I have seen a young woman levitate six feet off the ground and I have been in the presence of real, stinking, vile evil. If you're right and this house is as badly infected as you believe it to be, you could be putting your very soul in danger by coming back here, and mine as well. Are you sure you still want to proceed?"

Sister Immaculata had never been more certain of anything in her life. "Quite sure, Father."

Father Patrick sighed. "Well, if we're going to do this, we had better see if we can get in." He turned the handle of the front door. "Locked, I'm afraid."

"I tried to get hold of the landlord," the nun said, "but apparently he died last year. This property is all bound up with his estate. He didn't leave a will and it's going to be a long time until probate can be granted. There are quite a few family members scattered all over the world."

Father Patrick looked up at the boarded-up windows. "We won't get in through there, that's for sure."

Fear shot through Sister Immaculata. They couldn't give up,

especially not now since they were finally here. "But we must get in somehow. We must rid this place of the evil those girls let in. You read the newspaper reports. People around here are terrified. Stones keep being thrown. Windows are broken on an almost daily basis." She pointed at a nearby parked van bearing the name George Wainwright and Son, Glaziers. "The police are baffled because no one is ever seen throwing the stones. They seem to appear from nowhere."

"Sister, you know how hysterical the tabloid press can get. I said I have seen some strange phenomena in my life, but those instances are far outweighed by deliberate hoaxes, practical jokes and sheer delusion. No doubt someone, somewhere, is having a good laugh at everyone's expense. That's usually the way of it."

"Not if the devil is at work here." Sister Immaculata clutched the rosary in her pocket.

"Father?"

Sister Immaculata turned to see a young woman, dressed casually in jeans and T-shirt with a kitten motif.

"Yes, my child?" the priest replied.

"Have you come to exorcise the evil spirits from this house?"

The girl couldn't have been more than twenty. Dark circles under her eyes gave her an exhausted look and her hair probably hadn't been washed in weeks. It hung in greasy strings around her pinched, white face.

Sister Immaculata instinctively touched the girl's trembling hand with her own. "What have you seen, my dear?"

"Lights. Strange flickering lights. Figures dancing outside the back of the house. But they can't be there. They're dressed in old-fashioned clothes, but they're not real, are they? I can see straight through them. They're not...solid, like us."

"Does this happen regularly?" the priest asked.

The girl nodded, casting a fearful glance at the house. "Every month. And then there's the weird chanting. All sort of...echoey. No proper tune or anything. As if it's coming from another place."

"Like the radio?" Sister Immaculata asked.

The young woman shook her head. "No. Further than that.

I can't explain. Like it's coming down a tunnel from a long way away. Oh, I know that doesn't make any sense, but it's the best way I can describe it."

The nun looked to the priest for guidance and, hopefully, some explanation, but the young woman interjected before he had chance to respond.

"Then the stones come. Like hail sometimes. We've had our kitchen window smashed three times in the last year and now the insurance won't cough up."

"Father," Sister Immaculata said, "Now, surely you can see how important our mission is."

The priest coughed. "There still remains the problem of how to get into the house. We don't have a key. The front door's locked—"

"Then we should try the back door." The nun had already begun walking briskly down the road to the short alleyway which would take her to the back of the houses on Yarborough Drive. The priest and the young woman scurried after her.

"What is your name, child?" The priest was already out of breath trying to keep up with Sister Immaculata's steady canter.

"Rosalind," the girl said. "I live at number eight."

"And you can see the goings-on from there?"

"Yes. You'll see when we get there. There are no fences or walls between the houses. We just have our own yards. I've watched them from the kitchen."

They had reached the end of the alley and Sister Immaculata went left, maintaining her brisk pace. She turned into the untidy yard, overgrown with weeds and household rubbish blown in from neighboring properties.

"That's my house there." The girl pointed at an extension two doors down. It had a boarded-up window. "Of course, I can't see them anymore. Glad really. They scare me. There's real evil there."

They were outside number four and the young woman backed away. "I'll have to go. Got to pick up my little brother from school."

Before either of them could respond, the girl hurried away, back down the passage.

Sister Immaculata turned back to the business in hand. She pointed at the window on the left of the door. "Alice's room." The curtains were drawn open. Closer inspection revealed them to be coated in grime. Peering through the window, she saw debris, broken furniture and a bed that had seen far better days strewn around the once neat and tidy room. She stepped back to let Father Patrick take a look.

"Someone has had a fine old time wrecking this place and that's for sure," he said.

"Someone...or something."

The priest stared at her hard. Sister Immaculata broke eye contact. His gaze seemed to penetrate her soul.

"Sorry, Sister. I still have a problem with this. Let's see if this house is going to let us in."

He turned the handle of the back door. It too was locked, but this time with a simple Yale latch. Father Patrick rummaged in the pocket of his cassock and pulled out a piece of rectangular rigid plastic. "My bank card."

Sister Immaculata watched in mounting horror as the priest carefully inserted the card in the crack of the door and slid it gently upward while turning the handle.

"I used to be a prison chaplain," he said.

His explanation did nothing to reassure the nun who immediately offered up ten "Hail Marys" and an "Our Father". She crossed herself.

An audible click preceded the opening of the door.

"Always knew that would come in handy one day. An inmate told me how to do it after I arrived late for confession one day. I had locked myself out you see. Had to get a locksmith."

A chipped and dirty cup stood on the grime-covered draining board. Greasy dirt clung to the curtains and smeared the previously cream-colored walls. A smell of ancient cabbage and blocked drains sent bile shooting up into Sister Immaculata's mouth.

Father Patrick called to her from the hallway. "Sister, come along. We'd better not linger around. We have serious work to do."

The nun hurried after him into a hallway where dust

covered the tiled floor. She stopped as she caught sight of the devastation that had once been Vicky's room.

The door had fallen off its hinges and leaned drunkenly against the wall. As she and the priest peered inside, the ripped wallpaper, overturned and broken furniture and ragged curtains met their stunned gaze. They stepped inside.

A small book lay, somewhat incongruously, on an overturned chair. It had fallen open and, as she stood next to it, Sister Immaculata caught one line:

When death's darkest veil draws over you, then shall shadows weep.

She shuddered. Something about those words…

Father Patrick touched Sister Immaculata's hand. "Look at the floor."

Deep gouges raked across what remained of the floorboards. A gaping hole yawned wide in the middle of the room.

"Careful, Father," Sister Immaculata called as the priest took tentative steps to get a closer look. The floor creaked and the priest nearly lost his footing. He stopped near the edge of the hole.

"Holy Mary, Mother of God!"

"What is it, Father?"

The priest crossed himself and staggered backwards. "There's someone…something down there. Eyes. I saw eyes. Yellow. The devil's eyes." He tripped and fell, sprawling across the floor as he scrambled to get away from his own vision of hell.

A loud roar thundered from the hole. Sister Immaculata screamed. Something propelled her forward and she fell next to the priest. The two clung together.

"What was that, Father?"

"Something from hell itself."

A dark, opaque mist ascended, enveloping the two people in a sulfur-tainted shroud. Cries, as of souls in torment. Cackling laughter. Words in a language she couldn't understand assaulted her senses. Sister Immaculata clapped her hands to her ears. "Make it stop. Please, Father, make it stop."

Beside her. Father Patrick prayed.

The mist cleared a little, sufficiently enough that the nun could make out figures. Indistinct at first and then becoming human. Dressed in Edwardian clothes. Chief among them, a tall man with long, white hair. As the mist cleared still further, his pursed lips and cold, hard eyes penetrated her soul.

Sister Immaculata crawled backwards. She only made it a few inches before she hit a barrier. Behind her, a woman in a dark gray dress barred her way. Sister Immaculata glanced upward. The woman's head snaked down on a neck that lengthened like elastic. Inches away from her face, the woman's mouth opened, baring blackened teeth. It hissed at her, releasing stinking, poisonous breath.

"Mother of God!" The nun crossed herself and the head withdrew, the neck shrank. Raucous laughter replaced the serpentine hiss.

The mist had almost evaporated. It revealed a ring of men and women encircling the nun and the priest. Father Patrick's eyes were shut tight as his lips moved in fervent prayer.

The man with the white hair spoke. "You can stop the mumbo jumbo, priest. It will do you no good."

The priest's eyes shot open. He brandished a crucifix, thrusting it at the man. "Yea, though I walk through the valley of the shadow of death, I will fear no evil—"

In one swipe, the man tore the crucifix out of the priest's hand and flung it across the room.

"Where's your precious God now, priest?"

Father Patrick's face blanched. He struggled to stand.

"Let me help you."

Sister Immaculata watched in terror as some unseen force lifted the priest off the floor. He hung, suspended a few inches off the ground.

Father Patrick's lips trembled. "Hail Mary, full of grace—"

"*Enough.*" The man made a sweeping gesture with his right arm. The priest flew across the room and smashed against the wall. Bones cracked and snapped. He collapsed, unconscious, or dead. Sister Immaculata stared at the crumpled body. Every muscle in her body twitched.

The man laughed. "You do well to be afraid, Sister."

"Who are you?" she asked.

"Josiah Underwood. You are in my house and soon you will be one with us."

The nun crossed herself. "Never. As God is my witness."

"But He isn't, is He? *We* are your witnesses."

The group edged in closer, forming a tight ring around the nun. They began a deep, monotone chant and parted to allow their leader to pass through.

Sister Immaculata felt a scream start in the pit of her stomach. It worked its way up her gut and exploded from her mouth. Once she started, she couldn't stop. Across the room, through the gap made by the group, she saw the huddled shape of the priest quiver. What she saw next made her scream harder.

The priest's head jerked upward. He stared at her. But she didn't see *his* face. Impossibly, in a parody of himself, he smiled and stood. Then walked towards her. He stood over her.

"Now you see me, don't you, Sister?"

She saw it. But she didn't believe it. The voice was the priest's certainly, with its soft Irish brogue. But the face she stared at belonged to Josiah Underwood—his eyes transformed into a piercing, sickening yellow.

"Did you really think you would perform some stupid Catholic ritual and rid this house of me?"

"Where's Father Patrick? What have you done to him?"

The man laughed, a harsh, grating sound that tore through the nun.

"But you already know the answer to that, don't you, Sister? The evidence is here for you to see with your own eyes. I am he and he is me. We are inextricably joined together."

"That's not possible. Father Patrick—"

The voice dripped sarcasm. "I am your Father Patrick. Can't you see that?"

Sister Immaculata stopped trembling. She had to stare straight into the man's eyes. He commanded it. She sank deeper into the bilious, swirling pools where black, indistinct shapes wafted, draping themselves over her, dragging her in further away from reality. She looked down and saw she no longer wore her nun's habit. A black sweater and skirt reminded her of her old life before she entered the convent. The shadows enfolded her in their embrace, as she sank down into the darkness. The man's voice spoke to her.

"I had to bring you home, Anita. This is where you belong."

Chapter Nine
2019

I tried to moisten my dry mouth, but failed. "This isn't happening."

Suzie laughed. "Oh, but it is, Alice. There must always be thirteen. No more. No less. If the balance is altered, it must be made good again. We are the thirteen, and we are one."

"Make it stop, Suzie." Vicky pleaded, bursting into tears.

That did it. A rushing wave of anger swept through me and I made a dash for the door. A sound I had heard before stopped me. The walls heaved and expanded. I had my hand on the door handle, turned it and it came off in my hands. I leaped back, moments ahead of the door falling off its hinges and crashing to the floor.

"It's happening again," I yelled over the din of the howling gale which had erupted from nowhere. "The same as before. All those years ago."

Diana crouched on the floor, her hands over her ears. Vicky screamed like a fox in pain. Only the silent group in the middle seemed trapped in an invisible bubble, not a hair of their heads touched by the maelstrom of unholy wind.

Josiah Underwood spoke. "Look at your friends. No time has passed."

Vicky stopped screaming and Diana uncovered her ears. We each looked from one to the other.

The years had dropped away. My former housemates looked exactly as they did in 1972, even down to the clothes they wore. I looked down at my mini-skirt and platform shoes. I touched my hair. Long, thick, as it used to be. My joints no longer ached with the early stages of arthritis.

The wind stopped howling as abruptly as it had begun. Without a word, we three moved closer together. Suzie joined us and we linked hands in a circle.

"But there is one more of us," Suzie said. "Perhaps you didn't recognize her."

Anita stepped forward. Like us, she was dressed as she had been when I last saw her in 1972.

Josiah Underwood and the rest of his coven stood silently, watching us, as gradually we each began to acknowledge the truth. Suzie spoke and the strange words she said made sense at last.

"I told you I never left," she said. "What I haven't said is that you never left either. Only Anita, and we brought her back. Now the house is to be demolished, but we will remain. We will serve our master. We are the thirteen and we are one."

"But I remember my life after this house," I said.

"Do you, Alice? Are you sure about that?"

"Yes, I…" but, as I searched my brain yet again, I found nothing. No memories of anything since that day in 1972. I knew the years had passed, but I had no idea what had happened.

"I can't remember anything," Vicky said. "I must be going mad."

"If you are, so am I," Diana said, shaking her head.

Anita said nothing. She hadn't uttered one word since she had joined us.

"But…why?"

"Those memories you had were of your own invention," Suzie said. "You have slept for a long time. Now you are ready to serve."

"Serve?" A fresh wave of anger dispelled my fear. "I don't serve anyone."

Suzie smiled. "But you are so wrong, Alice. We all serve our master."

"What did you do to us all those years ago?" I demanded. "Murder us?"

"Released you," Suzie said, and that only served to incense me more.

"Released? We were *killed* in this house." Only when I said it did I realize for the first time what I had become—what all of us had become. What that evil bastard Josiah Underwood and his coven from hell had made us.

"Anita?" The girl acknowledged me for the first time. "How did you get back here?"

"I had to come," she said. "Before I took my vows as a nun, I had to try and make everything right here. I came with Father Patrick, but..." She shook her head and lowered her eyes.

I had concentrated my gaze on her and my companions. At some stage Josiah Underwood and the rest of his coven had left us. Only the five of us remained, in a circle, hands linked. I have no idea how long we stood there, silently.

It began slowly. A creeping gray mist that crawled along the floor, approaching us from all directions at once. As it neared us, it billowed and swirled as the gray became darker and we were completely enclosed.

We were in some sort of bubble, able to see each other clearly, but surrounded by the whirlpool of charcoal mist. No smell, no taste, no sound. I felt a strange calmness, but then it changed.

The mist parted and a shape emerged. Eliza Montague Jordan. For a moment, as she stood there, watching us, she looked as she must have in life. At first, her face was expressionless. Then, to my surprise, tears filled her eyes. I wondered then how many of Josiah Underwood's coven had joined willingly and how many had been coerced. Duped perhaps, with empty promises of eternal life—or else, enslaved.

Eliza's lips moved and I could hear her, not with my ears, but in my mind. I wondered if the others could, too. If so, they gave no indication of it.

"You read my words. 'The Darkest Veil'. It was meant for you, but you did not heed my warning. One day, the shadows will weep for *you*, Alice Lorrimer," she said, then vanished.

A rushing wind. Screams. Josiah Underwood looming over us. Eight feet tall. Dressed in purple robes with strange symbols. The gleam of a jeweled sword waved above us.

A growling, deep voice bellowed at us. "On your knees before your master."

More screams. Mine. Diana's. Vicky's.

A huge goat's head with massive curling horns replaced the head of Josiah Underwood. The walls fell away. A flock of ravens flapped over our heads.

We crouched, our arms over our heads, trying to protect ourselves. Shards of pain as the ravens' claws scratched. Then they were gone. Or transformed. A screeching parody of a choir, dressed in black, with gleaming yellow eyes, sang out of tune. Even the tune itself sounded discordant. The rushing wind blew into a screaming hurricane.

The voice almost deafened me. "You will serve your master."

We were back in the room again, its devastation all around us, but not for long. I looked around at the stunned faces of my old friends, Anita included. "I'm so sorry," I said. "It was all my fault."

"No, Alice," Anita said, her voice stronger than I had ever heard it. "I should never have left you with...*that*."

"And we could have refused to go through with the séance," Diana said.

"How do we get away?" I asked Anita, but I knew the answer.

"We don't. *This* is our destiny now."

The room shimmered and became the immaculate place it had been when we arrived. We too were transformed. I saw my friends' clothes morph into the gray, Edwardian dresses of the other women of the coven. I looked down and I now wore one, too. Anita was right. There could be no escape for us. Not one engineered by ourselves at any rate. Ghosts can't do that. Especially not cursed ones. Sometimes, I think back to my last real memories—1972, when the world and time stretched before me. Full of opportunity. Full of hope. All dashed on the rocks of folly.

When the Master summons us, we must obey. We emerge from our shadowy sleep where dreams of our previous lives ebb and flow, their truth as uncertain as shifting sands. Suzie is back with us. She is the friend we remember, since he returned her mind to her. We form ourselves into a circle around the being who used to be Josiah Underwood. He stands in his purple robes, the ancient symbols shimmer in gold—the Eye of Horus, crescent moons, stars, all adopted and abused by this monster before whom we must bow our heads.

He shows us his deeds. He is proud of his evil. Once, he showed us a vision of a city. Maybe Tokyo. Skyscrapers towered upward, cars jockeyed for position on clogged roads. Pedestrians hurried in all directions like worker ants. We chanted the words that he imprinted on our minds as we stood in a circle, each clasping the hand of our neighbor. I never know what the words mean. They are in some obscure long-dead language. Our voices rose. The Master raised his arms high, fists clenched. In the vision, the road began to tremble. People screamed and ran for cover as the sidewalks and roads cracked. Raised up. Created craters. Some men and women fell to certain death. Everywhere, glass shattered from windows. My spirit-self felt sickened. I tried to close my eyes, but this is not permitted. Our will is subjugated to his.

He needs us. He cannot perform his wickedness without us. When one of us passes into the light, he must replace the missing acolyte before he can regain his power. He takes what he needs. We do not see where they come from. They are not allowed to tell us. He performs his evil rites and we know that, somewhere in the world, tragedy has struck.

We, the thirteen, unlucky enough to pass too close within his sphere, can only link hands and recite the archaic, devilish chants.

Time has so little meaning now I have to accept what I am. The house crowds around us, its empty rooms echoing with the ghosts of our pasts. Eliza's book is lost in one of the rooms somewhere. If someone finds it, I hope they heed its warning and leave. Immediately. Before Josiah Underwood and his evil traps them with us, to wait until it is *their* turn to serve him.

My spirit is ever-fearful. I offer up a silent prayer, that someone will find a way to save us from the promised eternity of serving an evil, despicable master from hell. That my friends and I will find our way to the light, away from this limbo—caught between the living and the dead—and will grant us peace, so we may truly rest, as death's darkest veil shrouds us in its embrace.

Afterword
Two days later

"At least it's not raining, Del. You've got to be grateful for small mercies."

"It's all right for you, Gavin. You didn't grow up around here, with all the stories of ghosts and witches and stuff. This house is evil, I'm telling you. My parents told me. They used to live on the next street, back in the Seventies. Then four girls who were living here disappeared—three of them on the same day. No trace was ever found of them. Police searched the house from top to bottom. Nothing. They questioned the landlord, but he had been away at the time three of them went missing and there was no evidence to link him to any of the disappearances. Another girl who used to live here became a nun and returned here with a priest, apparently to try and exorcise the demons from this house. They both disappeared and no trace was ever found of them. At the same time this was all going on, the residents on this side of Yarborough Drive went through a reign of terror. Every night, windows smashed. They never caught anyone, and then it suddenly stopped."

Gavin, six feet tall in his socked feet and broad-shouldered, with a hint of the beer belly he would probably develop over the next ten years, shuddered.

Del snorted. "Superstitious bullshit."

"It's true, I'm telling you. The landlord couldn't rent any of the rooms in this house, it was so notorious. He gave up in the end. Boarded the place up. He had to do it himself because he couldn't get anyone brave enough to come and do it for him. He ended up in a mental home, so don't tell me it's all superstitious bullshit."

"Honestly, Gav, I never thought you of all people would
be reduced to a quivering jelly by an old, derelict house. How
many have you demolished? Hundreds I reckon. Come on, you
know the drill. Got to check all the rooms. Make sure no dossers or druggies are squatting. Then we'll get this baby down."

"You first," Gavin said, his attention drawn to a large black
bird with yellow eyes that seemed to be studying him from its
perch on a branch of a nearby rowan tree.

Del laughed and shook his head. "Wait 'til I tell the lads.
They'll never believe it. Gavin Hill scared of ghosts."

"Fuck off."

Del laughed harder. He fished in the pocket of his high-viz
jacket, brandished a key and opened the front door of number
four.

"What is that stench?" He pinched his nostrils. "Smells
like someone died in here."

Gavin muttered behind him. "I wouldn't be surprised."

"Let's get this over with. You check downstairs, I'll go up.
Don't forget the cellar. If anyone *is* here and they heard us,
they may have decided to hide down there."

Del kicked rubbish out of the way as he mounted the stairs,
his footsteps heavy in his boots.

Gavin took a deep breath and turned the handle of the first
door he came to. He was rewarded by the sight of an immaculate room, seemingly locked in a time capsule of the early
Seventies. It even smelled faintly of patchouli oil. Somehow
this felt more shocking than the awful stench in the hallway.
The wardrobe doors were shut. He strode over to them and
pulled them open. Empty.

He gave the room one more look and, with a shiver,
returned to the hallway. As he made his way over towards the
kitchen, crunching through debris and plaster, the smell grew
stronger. He came to another door on his right just before he
got there. He opened it. This time the room was as expected.
Wrecked. Torn curtains, broken furniture, stained and filthy
carpet. He didn't need to throw open the wardrobe in this

room, as the doors were on the floor anyway.

The kitchen stank so badly, he unlocked the back door and threw it open, taking gasps of the cool, fresh air. He turned back and made for the cellar door. Locked. He looked around. No sign of a key. Not the first time. Keys always seemed to go missing right when you needed them.

He gave the door a well-aimed and practiced kick. It shuddered. Two more thunderous kicks later and the wood splintered.

The thick, cloying stench nearly knocked him over. He retched, dashed outside and threw up in the yard.

Del joined him. "Nothing upstairs. God this fucking smell. Not surprised you got sick. Have you been down the cellar yet?"

Gavin, still retching, couldn't speak. He shook his head.

"Don't worry, I'll go." He left his mate. No more than a couple of minutes later, he came back, white-faced and shaking.

"Gavin, you're going to have to come down with me. I need a witness. And then we have to call the police."

"What?"

"Look, come with me. Now. Please." Del had already made it back to the kitchen, and Gavin staggered after him.

Faint daylight filtered in from a small window at yard level. On the floor, what looked like a jumble of old clothing had been stashed in a dimly lit corner, barely visible.

"Switch your torch on."

Gavin did so, as did Del, and the two beams shone over the mass of clothing.

Seconds passed before Gavin dared to believe what he saw. His torch reflected the white bones of a skeletal hand.

Del moved closer to the pile. "There's five of them. Five women by their dress."

He stepped back and fished in a pocket for his phone. He dialed the emergency services. "Police. I need to report a body— more than one. Women... By the looks of them, they've been here for years."

A sigh echoed through the cellar.

Gavin clutched his chest. A sharp pain snatched his breath away. It tore through his chest and down his left arm. Dead before he crashed onto the floor.

Del screamed into his phone for an ambulance, then knelt down beside the man he had known since childhood. Tears streamed down his face. Unseen by him, and wreathed in shadows, the pages of the discarded book rustled and it fell open at a well-thumbed page.

A whispered chant floated across the cellar.

"We are the thirteen, and we are one."

On the far side of the room, Josiah Underwood smiled and, in the shadows, five women wept.

About the Author

Cat first started writing when someone thrust a pencil into her hand. Unfortunately as she could neither read nor write properly at the time, none of her stories actually made much sense. However as she grew up, they gradually began to take form and, at the tender age of nine or ten, she sold her dolls' house, and various other toys to buy her first typewriter. She hasn't stopped bashing away at the keys ever since, although her keyboard of choice now belongs to her laptop.

The need to earn a living led to a varied career in sales, advertising and career guidance but Cat is now the full-time author of a number of supernatural, ghostly, haunted house and Gothic horror novels, novellas and short stories. For Crossroad Press these include: *The Devil's Serenade, Miss Abigail's Room, The Second Wife, Dark Avenging Angel, The Devil Inside Her, The Demons of Cambian Street* and *Cold Revenge*. She lives in Southport, in the U.K. with her longsuffering husband, and a black cat, who has never forgotten that her species was once worshiped in Egypt.

When not slaving over a hot computer, Cat enjoys wandering around Neolithic stone circles and visiting old haunted houses.

You can connect with her here:

www.catherinecavendish.com
https://www.facebook.com/CatherineCavendishWriter/
www.goodreads.com/author/show/4961171.Catherine_Cavendish

Curious about other Crossroad Press books?
Stop by our site:
http://store.crossroadpress.com
We offer quality writing
in digital, audio, and print formats.